Upon These Steps

Upon These Steps

David C. Reavis

Published by: David C. Reavis
Raleigh, N.C.
(www.UponTheseSteps.com)

CreateSpace Independent Publishing Platform
North Charleston, S.C.

Printed in the Unites States of America

ISBN: 1481074474
ISBN-13: 978-1481074476
(Paperback)

Library of Congress Control Number: 2012922680

DEDICATION

This book is dedicated to the loving memory of my parents:

James Lewis Reavis (1915-2009)

and

Lizzie Fay Howell Reavis (1916-1990)

Keepers of the Reavis Homeplace for over fifty years

"And their windows, and their arches, and their palm trees, were after the measure of the gate that looketh toward the east; and they went up unto it by seven steps; and the arches thereof were before them."

Ezekiel 40:22

ACKNOWLEDGMENTS

Much of the author's family research is based on original documents located in the North Carolina Office of Archives and History, and in the Vance County Clerk of Court Office; as well as family letters and oral family history.

Most of the events involving the chronicles of the NC Twenty-Third Regiment are based upon the *"History of the Twenty-Third Regiment,"* a manuscript written by Vines E. Turner, Assistant Quarter Master of the Regiment and H. Clay Wall, Sergeant of Company A of the Regiment, as written in Raleigh, NC on April 9, 1901; and subsequently published by the State in "Histories of the Several Regiments and Battalions from North Carolina in the Great War 1861-'65," Volume II, edited by Walter Clark.

Some of the events of the NC Twenty-Third Regiment are based on a collection of letters written by Private Jonathan Fuller Coghill to his family in Granville County; Part of the "Southern Historical Collection," housed at The University of North Carolina in Chapel Hill. Transcription by Betty Fuller of Raleigh, NC.

Many of the events (enlistment, furloughs, military pay, casualties, hospitalizations, captures, imprisonments, paroles, and exchanges, etc.) are based on the soldier's "Compiled Military Civil War Service Record," found on microfilm in either the National Archives or the NC Office of Archives and History.

Sources relating to the local history of Granville and Vance Counties include: *"Zeb's Black Baby,"* by Samuel T. Peace, Sr. in 1955, reprinted under the auspices of the Vance County Historical Society, Inc. in 1989; and public documents.

Source of quote attributed to Lewis Pleasant Reavis concerning his political views during the Presidential election of 1868 is from "Sketches" (abbreviated title), a privately printed manuscript written by Thurston Titus Hicks in 1926.

Special acknowledgement is given to various family members and genealogy researchers. This includes Samuel H. Allen (1882-1961), a recognized Reavis Family Historian from whom many other publications obtained their information.

Photos Courtesy of: 23rd Regimental Flag – North Carolina Museum of History; Private Samuel Wesley Reavis – Talmadge W. Reavis; Thomas and Bettie Reavis – Donald W. Reavis; Twins Ella and Della Reavis – Hazel Hughes Moore; Author's Picture and Uniform – Deelane Reavis; Cover Photos/Design – David C. Reavis.

Proofreading by: Marianne Gordey, Heather Hummer, and Norm Lambert.

Scripture verses are from the King James Version of the Holy Bible.

David C. Reavis

Chapter 1 – The Census Taker

It was the summer of 1860, and the census taker had visited most households in Granville County, North Carolina, the county located in the central piedmont of the State and bordering Virginia. Today was June 26 and was his day to visit the households along Glebe Road, an old stagecoach road that ran south to north, from the community known as Chalk Level toward Townesville. The road was bound by two tributary creeks: Indian Creek to the west and Anderson Swamp Creek to the east. Both creeks emptied into Nutbush Creek, which ultimately emptied into the Roanoke River.

The census taker had been looking forward to canvasing the households along Glebe Road, as he had heard much about two older houses along the road that intrigued him. The oldest house was Ashland, built in 1740 by Samuel Henderson. Samuel Henderson, along with his son Richard, helped organize the Transylvania Land Company, the company that commissioned Daniel Boone's expedition west to Kentucky. Ashland was very stately, resembling a typical southern plantation house. Ashland was now occupied by the Archibald Henderson family.

The other house along Glebe Road the census taker was anxious to visit was the Reavis House. Not as stately as Ashland, it was more of a modest farm house. The two-story framed Georgian style house had been built by the Samuel Reavis Family in 1789. Samuel had moved his family to Granville County from Northampton County, primarily for health reasons. His motive was to escape the lowlands that were conducive to sickness. The year 1789 was the same year that George Washington was inaugurated as President and the same year the University of North Carolina at Chapel Hill was founded. Samuel, who had been a patriot in the 14th Line of the Continental Army, arrived in Granville County with his wife Nancy, four sons, and six of his seven daughters.

Lewis Reavis, the eldest son of Samuel and Nancy, built a house just west of Chalk Level in Lonesome Valley, the highest point in the county. Chalk Level, a stagecoach stop, served as a dividing line similar to the Continental Divide. All creeks to the south of Chalk Level ran into the Tar River, while all creeks to the north ran in the opposite direction into the Roanoke River. In 1836, Lewis donated ten acres of his land to entice the Raleigh and Gaston Railroad to put a train station in Lonesome Valley instead of Chalk Level. This act contributed to the growth that later sprang the town of Henderson in 1841. Considered the town's founder, the name of the town was almost named Reavisville. However, Lewis insisted that it be named for his recently departed friend, Judge Leonard Henderson.

The six daughters of Samuel Reavis all married into Granville County families. Two of the sons, Thomas and Whitfield, both initially built houses at Chalk Level. Whitfield, whose first name was actually William, operated the Reavis Tavern before moving to Lonesome Valley where he became the postmaster. Thomas was a constable for a short time before heading west to Tennessee. The fourth son, Samuel Jones Reavis, built along Glebe Road in the area known as the Silver Spring Community. It was the house built by Samuel Jones Reavis that the census taker would visit today.

As the census taker approached the Reavis House sitting up on the hill, he could not help but notice the two rows of cedar trees that ran away from the front of the house. The two rows were not parallel to each other, as one would expect trees to be in front of a Southern plantation. Instead, the two rows of cedars met at the front of the house and formed a forty-five degree angle, more like a compass. One row was along the dirt pathway that led directly east toward Greystone Community, and the other row along the dirt pathway that led south-east toward Chalk Level. Within the two rows, near the apex where the house stood, were two huge boxwood bushes. The bushes must have been at least eight feet tall.

Striking to the eye were three stone chimneys that graced the house, casting a silhouette against the clear blue sky. He later learned that the chimneys serviced five different fireplaces in the house. One chimney alone serviced three fireplaces, one in the cellar, one on the first floor, and one on the second floor. He learned that the fireplace in the cellar was where the slaves did most of the cooking.

The census taker's next observation was the magnificent rock steps in front of the house. The five-foot-high steps were shaped almost like a half-pyramid, but circular. The base of the steps was about eighteen feet wide. The steps narrowed as they went up, with one single rock at the top. As the census taker approached the steps, a jack rabbit, which had been sitting on the first step, hopped to the ground. With somewhat of a moderate speed, the rabbit ran toward the family cemetery which was north of the house, about 100 yards away. As the census taker walked up the steps, he counted each row of steps, seven in all.

However, it was the single half-oval rock at the top that really grabbed his attention. It was about five feet wide where it was attached to the porch, and about three feet in depth. Through the middle of the rock, from one side to the other, ran a dark streak, about three inches wide. The census taker had seen many unique rock formations. However, this was the first time he had ever seen a rock that looked as if a petrified water vein were running through it.

Before the census taker could step up onto the porch, a striking middle-age woman appeared at one of the doors that opened onto the porch. This was also interesting, as the house had not one, but two front doors. The woman appeared to be in her mid to late 40s. She was tall and slender, and was wearing a bonnet. Her dress appeared to have been crafted from feed sacks obtained from a grist mill. Although her face looked weathered, she had the warmest smile the census taker had seen in weeks.

"How are you today?" he asked.

"Fairly middling." She replied.

"Are you the lady of the house?" He then asked.

"I am." She replied, in a cautious manner. "What may I have the pleasure of your visit?"

"I am the census taker. As you may know, the U.S. Constitution mandates that a census be taken every ten years. I hope this is a good time for my visit?"

Mary had been expecting the visit, as she was aware that the census taker had been canvasing the houses along the road that week. "Yes, it's as good as any. My name is Mary

Coghill Reavis. I live here with my husband, Lewis Pleasant Reavis, and six of our children. Two of our children are married and on their own now."

The census taker seemed to be more interested in the house than who lived there. He remarked, "You know, a census has been taken every ten years since 1790. That's about the time this house appears to have been built, is it not?"

Mary responded, "Yes, the house is some seventy years old now. It was built by my husband's father, Samuel Jones Reavis. Well, he only supervised the building of it. The laborers were actually slaves. At the time of his death in 1854, he and his wife Martha Patsey Harris owned thirty-four slaves. Patsey has been dead ten years now, while Samuel has only been dead six years. My husband Lewis inherited 300 of the 2,000 plus total estate acres. The tract extends from Anderson Swamp Creek all the way to Indian Creek. The other ten brothers and sisters inherited the remainder of the estate."

The census taker remarked, "I can see that it took some doing just to build these steps. It must have been a feat similar to the building of the Egyptian Pyramids. It surely took real craftsmen to haul them here and so precisely fit them into place. The steps are truly one of the unknown architectural wonders of Granville County."

"Yes," Mary replied, "Family legend has it that the seven steps are patterned after the seven steps referenced in the 40th Chapter of Ezekiel. The top step with the water vein running through it represents the Living Waters referenced by Jesus Christ in the Book of John. Also, you will notice that the steps face east, the direction from which Jesus will return one day to gather His elect. You will also notice that the graves in the family cemetery adjacent to the house face the east as well. This will facilitate the taking up of those who are asleep in the graves when He comes." Mary then quoted Matthew 24:27, "For as the lightning cometh out of the east, and shineth even unto the west; so shall also the coming of the Son of man be."

Mary continued, "The cedar trees represent the Cedars of Lebanon, used in the building of King Solomon's Temple. There are other symbolic meanings to the angle and placement of the steps in reference to the cedars, but my husband has not relayed them to me, apparently some type of secret. Also, since the house does not have a central entrance hallway, two front doors were designed to provide a sense of symmetry and balance, key ingredients to humanity and relationships."

The census taker then asked, "How about those two boxwood bushes?"

"Oh! They were planted in 1790 in memory of Papa Samuel Jones Reavis and his wife Martha Patsey Harris Reavis. They are nearly eight feet tall now. However, it is anticipated they will live another 1,000 years and should reach the height of about 15 feet. Like our family, they will weather all storms that may come our way. On the practical side, there are some medicinal purposes of the leaves and the sawdust from the wood. Some of the uses include treatment of toothaches, fever, stomach aches, and rheumatism. The leaves also help promote hair growth, even on our horses."

The census taker then asked, "Tell me then, what's the meaning of that covered well in the back yard? Surely there must be one."

Mary replied, "Oh. There's no special meaning. It's where we get our drinking water and where we sit to eat watermelons. It's nearly 60 feet deep and not quite three feet in diameter. The walls are comprised of rocks. Suspended from the well's roof is a pulley and bucket used to draw water. Papa Samuel used his divining gift to locate the spot to dig the well. Before he died, Papa taught my husband how to take a branch from a peach tree to use as a divining rod. The well does remind me though of Jacob's well, where Jesus forgave the Samaritan woman of her sins and promised to give her Living Water."

Beginning to feel the summer heat, Mary then said, "Come into the house out of the sun. I'll treat you to some cold apple cider, made from apples gathered from our orchard." Southern hospitality was extended to the census taker throughout the process of providing him with the names and ages of the eight members of the household: Lewis Reavis – Head of household, age 55; Mary – Wife, age 46; Thomas – Son, age 20; Sam – Son, age 18; Arella –Twin Daughter, age 16; Della – Twin Daughter, age 16; John Billie – Son, age 10; Mary – Daughter, age 8.

"There are three last things I need to complete the census. Did the children attend school during the year, and what's the value of your real estate and of your personal property?"

About that time, Mary's husband came into the house, having been in the fields supervising the slaves. "I'll have to let Lewis answer those questions." Mary told him. After brief introductions and courtesies were exchanged, Lewis responded to the last questions, "All six children attended school during the year. The two older brothers, Thomas and Sam, went to the Male Academy in Henderson. The other children went to the one-room Wortham School up the road near Chalk Level. Regarding the value questions, considering all the acreage, the Real Estate value would be $6,000. Considering the household furniture, the farm implements, and the 17 slaves owned (14 blacks and 3 mulattos), the personal property would be $19,800."

With all his questions having been answered, the census taker was about to leave. He could hear the twin girls and their two younger siblings playing in the back yard around the well, along with several hunting dogs. He assumed the two older sons were in the fields working or doing chores. Little did he know that they were actually down at the millpond with some neighboring boys. Girls were not allowed at the pond, as the boys sometimes went skinny dipping there.

Before leaving, the census taker inquired about the two grown children who were no longer living in the home. Mary said, "Oh you will likely get to meet our daughter Lucy today. She lives with her husband Alex Wortham in the overseer house, just a piece up the path from our house. Lucy is 22 years old now, having moved out three years ago when she got married. I assume you will be taking their census next."

"You will likely also be visiting our twenty-five year old daughter Martha and her husband John Vaughan. Martha moved out six years ago. It seems our house is not as crowded since the girls moved out. However, they do visit quite often, at least weekly. Next to godliness and cleanliness, family loyalty is of upmost importance."

The census taker left the Reavis House with a warm feeling, having experienced a family that seemed to be well blessed, both economically and spiritually. Sometimes life seems to be all rosy, with few cares. Little did any of them know that before the next census would be taken ten years later in 1870, the family would face hardships that tongues would be hard to tell.

Chapter 2 – Christmas of 1860

Six months had passed since the census taker had visited the Reavis House on Glebe Road. Today was Christmas Day 1860, the seventy-second Christmas celebrated in the Reavis House. By this time of year, the harvest had been completed. The tobacco had been cropped, cured, stripped, and taken to market. The corn had been picked and shucked, with some having been taken to the grist mill and some stored in the crib out back. There was enough flour and grain for cooking to last a year and enough corn to feed the livestock for a year. The slaves had picked the cotton, which brought a good price at the cotton gin. There was sufficient food in the pantry, with vegetables from the garden having been preserved during the summer months. Chickens were producing eggs daily.

The smokehouse was getting a little bare, as there had not been a hog killing since January, eleven months earlier. However, there was enough smoke-cured ham and fatback to have a Christmas feast. There was no concern about eating the last ham in the smokehouse. This was because the next hog killing would take place within the next several weeks, as soon as there was an extended cold spell. Farm families knew they had to wait until temperatures were below forty degrees to prevent the meat from spoiling when they slaughtered hogs.

It was only six o'clock in the morning, and yet excitement was already stirring in one of the upstairs bedrooms, the one where the twin girls slept, along with their younger sister Mary. The teenaged twins, Ella and Della, had taken on the responsibility of caring for the eight-year old Mary. This took a burden off mother, who had a handful with the ten-year old son John Billie. The girls knew that presents would be waiting for them downstairs. They were eager to go down the steep enclosed staircase, which had a door at the bottom that was normally kept closed.

John Billie, who slept downstairs, was just as excited as his sister Mary. Sam on the other hand, who slept in the other upstairs bedroom, was not quite as anxious to go downstairs. For over seventeen years, Sam had shared the bedroom with his older brother Thomas, who had recently moved out. This was because, on December 5, Thomas married his sweetheart Bettie Waddie Best of Warren County. One of the things Sam missed was seeing Thomas asleep on his back with his right leg bent so that his knee arched up in the air. This was a trait common among many Reavises, including the females.

While the twins thought they knew who Saint Nicholas really was, young Mary and John Billie were at the ages where they were beginning to have doubts. The night before, Mary had asked her father if there really was a Saint Nick. Her father had sat both Mary and John Billie down and told them, "Children, I really cannot tell you if there is a Saint Nick or not, because I've never read about him in the Bible. However, I can tell you that there *is* a Jesus, because whatever we read about in the Bible you can count on it being the truth." This was the father's way of being truthful. He also knew that many children, once upon figuring out that there was not a Saint Nick, sometimes stopped believing that Jesus was real. This was because children sometimes put Jesus in the same category as Saint Nick and the Tooth Fairy. Lewis did not want his children to arrive at this false assumption.

Regardless of their understanding of the truth about Saint Nick, all the children, as instructed by their mother, had put talcum powder on their toes before they went to bed Christmas Eve. Mother had told them that when Saint Nick came, he would smell their toes to see if they were asleep or not. These were the same instructions Mary's mother Lucy Coghill had told her when she was a little girl.

Normally, the slaves would have built fires in the downstairs fireplaces by this time. However, Lewis had done this chore today, as it was tradition that the slaves were relieved of their servant duties on Christmas. Although the temperature was in the twenties in the upstairs bedrooms, the children who slept upstairs were warm, as they all slept under several quilts that their mother had made. Yet the fireplace was the first place they ran to once they descended the stairs.

Breakfast was to be delayed, as all gathered around the cedar Christmas tree that stood in the corner of the parlor. The seven-foot tree only reached half way to the ceiling. While the ceiling was fourteen feet high, the doors leading into the parlor were only five and one-half feet high. The taller boys always had to duck their heads as they entered the room. The tree was adorned with a few ornaments, most being homemade. Several were made of corks that had come from wine bottles.

Hanging from the mantle over the fireplace in the parlor were five stockings, one for each child still living in the household. In each of the stockings the following items were found: apples, pecans, and hard rock candy. Lewis had often joked that he was going to cut holes in the toes of the children's stockings and place a box under them to catch whatever may fall out for him. It was always exciting for them to discover the treasures inside the stockings.

There were other gifts under the tree, some wrapped and some not. Sam got a long-awaited Bowie knife. John Billie got a hand-carved wooden pistol and a ball. The three girls each received several ribbons for their hair and a pretty lace-trimmed handkerchief.

Lewis had secretly carved a new large bread bowl for Mary. Also, while on one of his trips to Raleigh, he had traded one of his prized hogs for a beautiful cameo brooch to give her.

During the year, Mary had sold hen eggs and squirreled away the money to buy Lewis a gold pocket watch. She had a jeweler in Oxford to engrave it. "Lewis Reavis -1860" was engraved on the outside cover. On the inside cover was the following engraving: "This too shall pass!"

Around 11 o'clock, through the back door walked daughter Lucy and her husband Alexander Wortham. They had walked, as their house was only 300 yards up the dirt path to the west. They came through the door with some pep in their steps and holding hands. Although they had been married three years now, one would think they were still on their honeymoon. Lucy was 19 when she had married Alex, who was 21 at the time. They did not yet have any children.

Not far behind Lucy and Alex, the newly wedded Thomas and Bettie arrived, also by foot. Their house was on the eastern side of Glebe Road, as Thomas had taken on the responsibility of tending the crops along Anderson Swamp Creek. It was their first visit to the Reavis House since they married just two weeks earlier. They acted as if they were still courting.

Shortly after Thomas and Bettie's arrival, a clatter was heard in the front yard. The twins ran to the front door to see who it was, as they were anticipating the arrival of their two nieces. When they opened the door, they could see a one-horse wagon coming up the dirt path along the row of cedar trees. The opening of the door scared off the jack rabbit that had been squatting on the bottom of the circular rock steps. The rabbit scurried toward the cemetery.

Sure enough, in the wagon the twins could see their older sister Martha and her husband John Vaughan. Martha had married John six years earlier in the spring of 1854 when she was 19 years old. John, being somewhat older than Martha, was actually twice her age, having been born in 1815. Sitting between them on the wagon bench was a toddler, who was not quite three years old. In Martha's lap, wrapped in a blanket like a pig, was a five-week old baby girl. The toddler's name was Nora, short for Elenora. The baby's name was Belle.

As they walked up the circular rock steps, Martha stopped on the top step, the one with the petrified water vein running through it. Martha looked down at Belle whom she was holding in her arms, pulled the blanket away from her face, and said to her, "Belle, this is your first Christmas and the first time up these steps to your MaMa and PaPa's house. You are truly blessed to have such loving grandparents. We trust you will have many happy days playing on these steps, just as I did when I was a child."

Christmas dinner was served at noon. Southern families normally referred to the noon meal as dinner, and the evening meal as supper. After putting food on their plates, the younger children were seated at a separate table in the parlor. The adults sat around a table in the dining room. The food had been cooked in cast iron pots hanging in the fireplace in the cellar.

Before partaking of the food, Lewis asked everyone to bow their heads for grace. His prayer included praise to God and acknowledgment of the reason for the season, the celebration of the birth of their Savior. He also made a remembrance of those family members who were no longer with them and had gone on to their reward. He mentioned his parents Samuel and Patsey Reavis, and his wife Mary's parents, Thomas and Lucy Coghill. Both sets of parents had died within the past ten years. However, Lewis wanted the family to know the importance of the scripture he often quoted, "Honor thy father and thy mother: that thy days may be long upon the land which the LORD thy God giveth thee."

Lewis also mentioned the memory of the infant daughter of Martha and John, who had died three days after being born in October 1856. The death of their first grandchild was the major event up to this point that had tested the faith of Lewis and Mary Reavis. Other than this death, life appeared to be rather rosy for them. All five of these deceased individuals were buried in the family cemetery adjacent to the house.

After the 'Amen,' Mary spoke up and gave her annual Christmas message, the same one she had given every previous Christmas, "Family, there are many a happy child today, and many a sad one." She paused before continuing, "Also, there are many people here this Christmas who will not be here next Christmas."

The family knew they were being reminded that they should be grateful for what they had. Mary frequently quoted the scripture, "In everything give thanks: for this is the will of God in Christ Jesus concerning you."

The family also knew that they were being reminded to treat each other with Christ-like love, as we never know when we may not have them with us any longer.

They then all dug in and enjoyed their meal, thankful for their many blessings and not seemingly being concerned with any troubles of the world.

After the meal, Lewis opened his new pocket watch to check the time. Upon see the engraving –"This too shall pass!" - it stuck him that these good times would not last forever.

Chapter 3 – Eve of War

The confrontation came to a head in the early morning of April 12, 1861 in Charleston Harbor. The State of South Carolina had already seceded from the Union and had given notice for the Union forces to evacuate Fort Sumter. Upon refusing to evacuate, throughout the night the Confederate Army bombarded the fort with continuous cannon fire. Although the Federalists returned fire with their limited number of cannons, they were significantly outgunned. The following day, U.S. Major Robert Anderson was forced to surrender the fort and evacuate his Union troops. The ensuring Civil War would sometimes be referred to as the War Between the States, and in some Southern circles, the War of Northern Aggression. Regardless of what it was called, in many cases it would pit brother against brother and neighbor against neighbor.

In the debates and arguments that transpired during the years leading up to the war regarding possible secession, North Carolina took a back seat to the outspoken South

Carolina. It was years of political conflict characterized by political speeches and numerous newspaper editorials that eventually ignited secession.

Contrary to the sentiment in most of the Southern states, in North Carolina there was a growing protest against the slavery system and the associated inequalities. This sentiment was more prevalent among the non-slaveholding citizens and was reflected in the words of Zebulon Vance. Zeb Vance was serving as U.S. Senator from the State when he stated, "Seven-tenths of our people owned no slaves at all, and to say the least of it, felt no great and enduring enthusiasm for its [slavery's] preservation, especially when it seemed to them that it was in no danger."

Senator Vance would later change his sentiment and become the Governor after the State eventually seceded and became a part of the Confederacy.

While the majority of the citizens in North Carolina had a disdain for the institution of slavery, there was a strong state-rights minority made up primarily of planters in the eastern part of the State that exerted their influence in the legislature and in the press to promote their agenda. This minority group insisted that secession was not only a right of the states, but perhaps a remedy. The firing on Fort Sumter fueled the group's position. It was not until President Lincoln's requisition on the State for troops after the firing on Fort Sumter did the governor, legislature, and majority of the citizens come to the conclusion that secession was the only option. The alternative was to engage in fighting against sister Southern states.

Upon receiving the news of the April firing on Fort Sumter, Lewis Reavis knew that the dark clouds of war were about to roll in and threaten the prospects of his family's peace and happiness as they then knew it. Lewis's two oldest sons, Thomas and Sam, saw his dismay and asked him his thoughts on slavery. Lewis responded and told them that his views were generally the same as those of Robert E. Lee, a West Point graduate and currently a General in the Union Army. Lewis reached into a desk drawer and pulled out a copy of a letter dated December 27, 1856. The letter had been written by Lee in response to a speech given by the then President Pierce. Lewis continued, "Sons, let's go out and sit on the front steps."

Upon sitting down, Lewis read them excerpts from the letter: "There are few, I believe, in this enlightened age, who will not acknowledge that slavery as an institution is a moral and political evil....How long their servitude may be necessary is known and ordered by a merciful Providence. Their emancipation will sooner result from the mild and melting influences of Christianity than from the storm and tempest of fiery controversy. This influence, though slow, is sure."

Placing the letter in his pocket, Lewis Reavis looked into the eyes of the two boys listening intently to his every word and told them, "Sons, there are some things that we have no control over. We must trust that the providence of God will prevail and eventually allow all men to be free. Just as General Lee indicated in his letter five years ago, slavery as an institution is a moral and political evil. His hopes were that Christianity would eventually prevail."

Thomas then asked, "How long will we have to wait?"

Lewis responded, "Unfortunately, we must endure whatever process God chooses to accomplish His sovereign will. Regardless, we all will play a part in the process that will be thrust upon us, whether we like it or not. We will all likely be called upon to sacrifice economically, and perhaps even with life. In any event, we must seek God's guidance, and endure. Any suffering and sacrifice we endure will pale to that experienced by Jesus Christ."

Sam then asked, "If we go to war, whose side do you think God will be on?"

Lewis pondered for a second and then responded, "Son, the question should not be whose side will God be on, but will we be on God's side?"

Within five weeks of the firing on Fort Sumter, the North Carolina legislature indeed did pass a resolution calling for secession. Like it or not, Granville County along with the rest of the counties in North Carolina were at war, and the Reavis household would never be the same.

Chapter 4 – Train Depot Gathering

One day after learning of the State's secession from the Union, many of the county's citizens had gathered at the train depot in Henderson, which is where the resolution was posted. The train depot was located on ten acres of land that Lewis Reavis, the oldest son of Samuel and Nancy Reavis, had donated to the Raleigh and Gaston Railroad in 1836. Such a move allowed Lewis to turn his house into a hotel to accommodate the travelers.

Lewis had married Sarah Wyche, daughter of Peter Wyche and Elizabeth Jenkins, who lived on the Tar River. Members of the Wyche family were well-educated, with many of them becoming doctors and dentists. Several of the doctors served in the Confederate Army, caring for the many wounded on the battlefields. Benjamin Wyche was most known for being President of the Raleigh and Gaston Railroad.

Most individuals at the railroad depot gathering were young men curious about the possibility of joining the

Confederate Army, which was seeking volunteers to join the cause. The Confederacy would not enact a Conscription Act until a year later in April of 1862. The first act would apply to all healthy white men between the ages of 18 and 35, requiring a three-year service. The act did however have a provision that allowed for substitutions. All men who had previously voluntarily enlisted for a one-year term would have their enlistment period extended for an additional three years.

The Second Conscription Act would raise the upper threshold age to 45. The substitution provision would later be repealed. By the third year of the war, the Third Conscription Act would put the age thresholds at between 17 and 50. The lower threshold age of 17 in 1864 would affect those boys who were only 14 when the war started.

Brothers Thomas and Sam Reavis, as well as their brother-in-law Alex Wortham, were among the curiosity seekers inquiring about the all-volunteer army. Enlistments longer than one year seemed unnecessary, as most thought the Confederates would surely defeat the Yanks within that time. This was an illusion of many Southerners, including Confederacy President Jefferson Davis.

Thomas, Sam, and Alex were motivated when they saw a number of their cousins at the train depot. They counted three Reavis cousins: George James Reavis, James Robert Reavis, and William Amis Reavis. Little did they know at the time that James Robert would later enlist in the Warren Guards and serve three years before being killed at the Battle of Spotsylvania Court House on May 11, 1864. George and William would both be more fortunate than James Robert, as they would later enlist as well, but would survive the war.

James Robert Reavis was a distant cousin to several prominent individuals. This connection was on his mother Charity High Hunt's side. They included: Sarah Knox Taylor, the first wife of President Jefferson Davis; Confederate General Richard Taylor; President Zachary Taylor; President James Madison; and John Penn, signer of the Declaration of Independence.

Five of the Parham Family cousins were at the train depot as well. The cousins, who were all grandchildren of Lewis W. Parham and wife Lucy Reavis, were: Asa C. Parham, James Arthur Williamson Parham, Samuel Jones Parham, Thomas Buckner Whitfield Parham, and William Asa Gaston Parham.

In addition, four brothers of the Coghill Family from Kittrell were in the crowd: Jonathan Fuller Coghill, Kenchen Wesley Coghill, James Norfleet Coghill, and Joseph Wily Coghill. Their uncle James T. Stone was tagging along with them.

Thomas, Sam, and Alex were surprised to see their neighbor Frank McCraw, Jr. at the depot. Frank was a first cousin on their mother's side. Frank and his wife of five years, Bettie Wiggins of the Spring Valley Community, lived in the household adjacent to the Reavis House. Frank had already endured many family trials - having to deal with his father being declared insane and having to take care of his elderly mother after his father's death. Frank would eventually be drafted, and unfortunately, be killed at Cedar Creek, Virginia in 1864. A plot of ground beneath a pecan tree in the Reavis Family Cemetery, beside his grandparents Thomas and Lucy Coghill, would eventually be the final resting place of the remains of Frank, Jr. A jack rabbit would frequently be seen around his grave.

A future brother-in-law of Thomas and Sam, John Jeremiah Pegram, was also at the train depot. John Jeremiah was the boyfriend of the twin named Ella.

After a large crowd had gathered at the train depot, a spirited and inspiring speech expounding the Southern cause of states' rights was given by Charles Christopher Blacknall, the owner and operator of the Mineral Springs Hotel in Kittrell. Blacknall was organizing a company of volunteers to be known as the Granville Rifles.

Like a spirited crusader, C.C. Blacknall stirred the enthusiasm of Southern loyalty among the listeners. In his raised right hand he had a rolled-up piece of paper, waiving it like a sword. While not needing a prompter for his speaking points, the paper contained excerpts from the "Nutbush Paper." This document had been written by George Sims almost a hundred years earlier, an address which helped spur support for the revolution against the King's tyranny. Blacknall gave several quotes from the paper pertaining to "those absolute rights which we are entitled to as men....and to throw off the heavy yoke, which is cast upon our necks, and resume our ancient liberties and privileges, as free subjects."

Like the Sims paper, Blacknall's address was a compelling speech intended to draw on the emotions of the residents of Granville County, espousing the cause of freedom, family, and the Southern way of life.

After hearing the speech, Sam, Thomas, Alex, and Frank returned to their respective homes on Glebe Road. They each struggled with the decision to volunteer or not. The only one of the four who would initially accept the call to volunteer was Sam, age 17, the youngest of the group. Thomas and

Alex would both wait a year to enlist, when the first Confederate Conscription Act would provide them no other choice. Frank McCraw would wait two years before he enlisted in November of 1863, at the age of 29. Thomas' decision not to volunteer at this time was affected partly to him having learned that week that his wife Bettie was experiencing morning sickness, indications of a possible pregnancy.

The spring of 1861 marked the beginning of an era that would shed a dark cloud over the Reavis House, one that would test the faith and grit of the family members, to the extent no one could imagine. Not even the five fireplaces could provide sufficient warmth that would offset many of the cold nights to follow.

Chapter 5 – Talking Frogs

Arriving at the Reavis House on Glebe Road after the train depot gathering, Sam ascended the front circular steps, seemingly in deep thought. Out of the corner of his eye, Sam saw three frogs, each sitting on different steps. Sam paused and looked at each frog as he reached the step upon which they sat. To Sam, it appeared as if each one of the frogs was staring him straight in the eye. Sam chuckled to himself and went on inside the house.

Sam had been born July 18, 1843, with the given name of Samuel Wesley Reavis. In later years, he would go by the name of S.W. Reavis. Sam had a somewhat different personality than his older brother Thomas. While Thomas was a "romantic," showing interest in girls, Sam was more of an "adventurer." The census taker had mistakenly recorded Sam's age as 18 the previous June. However, Sam was now still only 17, one month shy of being 18.

Sam tossed and turned that night as he attempted to go to sleep in the upstairs bedroom. He could not help from thinking about the arousing speech that C.C. Blacknall had given that day at the train depot. The prospect of serving in the Confederate Army with fellow glory seekers brought out a high level of exhilaration in him. Being a hot summer night, the two hinged windows were wide open in order to get a breeze. Outside he could hear crickets and tree frogs. After about an hour, he finally dozed off to sleep.

Sam then had the strangest dream he ever had. In the dream, he saw three frogs, the same ones he saw that afternoon on the front steps. Strangely enough, the frogs could talk. Each frog had a name. Instinctively, Sam knew that each frog represented a family relative that his father had told him about as a boy.

The first frog croaked and said, "Sam, my name is Blackbeard." Upon hearing the frog's name, Sam had a recollection of a story his father had once told him. The daughter of Samuel and Nancy Reavis who did not relocate with the family to Granville County in 1789 had married Hartwell Hyde. Instead, Mary and Hartwell moved from Northampton County directly to Tennessee. Hartwell's grandfather was Richard Hyde, a pirate and member of Blackbeard's gang. In the dream, Sam saw himself on board Edward Teach's *Queen Anne's Revenge*. The ship was engaged in a fight with another ship, the *Black Pearl*. Sam saw himself in a sword fight and was enjoying it.

The second frog croaked and said, "Sam, my name is Indian Trader." Upon hearing the frog's name, Sam had a recollection of another story his father had once told him. Richard Hyde quit his life of piracy when Blackbeard was killed in 1718. He then became a licensed Indian Trader. While escorting the Superintendent of Indian Affairs through Creek Territory, both the Superintendent and Hyde were severely beaten and disfigured (ears clipped off) by some Creek warriors when they were caught in bed with the Indians' wives. Although having lost parts of their ears, the two men felt fortunate that their loss was not worse, considering their crimes. In the dream, Sam saw himself fighting Indians. As a group of Indians rode by him on their horses, Sam shot the riders off, one by one. Sam was elated that he could not miss with his musket.

The third frog croaked and said, "Sam, my name is Alamo." Upon hearing the frog's name, Sam again had a recollection of a third story his father had once told him. Samuel and Nancy Reavis' son named Thomas, who had come with the family to Granville County in 1789, eventually moved on to Tennessee. One of Thomas' sons was named James Blount Reavis. In the spring of 1836, James Blount went with Davy Crocket to Texas to fight with the Texas Army. Upon arriving at the Alamo, the men discovered that James Blount was under-aged. Just two days before the Mexicans laid siege, the men all agreed that James Blount should be sent home, as he was too young of a lad to die. In the dream, Sam saw himself on the top of the north wall of the Alamo. He was standing between Davy Crocket and Jim Bowie as Santa Anna attacked. Sam was proud to be fighting with two of his heroes.

The next morning, Sam was awakened by the sound of a crowing rooster, clearly heard through the open windows. As he shuffled down the enclosed staircase, he noticed the sword of his great grandfather Samuel Reavis hanging on the wall, near the bottom of the steps. Having enlisted in May of 1775, the elder Samuel had served in the Continental Line for two and one-half years. During his last two years, he served in

"His Excellency Guards" for North Carolina's first Governor, Richard Caswell. At the time, Tryon Palace in New Bern served as the State's Capitol. Sam had passed the sword many times during his boyhood, but today he noticed that it was swinging slightly, from side to side as he passed it.

The family had breakfast as usual, comprised of eggs, grits, fatback, biscuits with molasses, and milk. The milk had a taste of onion, as there was still a good crop of spring onions in the pasture for the cows to eat. The onion taste always showed up in the milk when the cows were milked during the spring months.

After breakfast, Sam told his father that he needed to talk with him. They went out and sat in two of the rocking chairs on the front porch. As they sat down, a jack rabbit that had been sitting on the bottom level of the circular steps ran off toward the cemetery. While the beagles in the yard were good hunting dogs, for some reason they never bothered any of the rabbits around the house or cemetery.

Lewis instinctively knew what his son Sam wanted to talk about, as Lewis knew his sons pretty well, perhaps better than they knew themselves. Sam had always had an adventurous spirit, and Lewis knew that this day would one day come.

"Father, you know how the Federalists are boasting about their superiority." Sam said. "They would destroy the rights of the South and our way of life. My friends are hankering to go fight and for me to join them." Sam stopped before he could ask the question if he could go, but his eyes said it all.

Without looking at Sam, Lewis leaned over the side of the porch, spit out a wad of tobacco juice, and asked a question, "Have you prayed about this matter?"

"Yes, Father, I have been for several weeks." Sam replied. "In my heart, I believe I need to go." No one knows if Sam's cardinal desires, which were carved by his adventurous spirit, were in line with or overshadowed by whatever the will of God had for Sam. Yet, family beliefs were that God would be with him regardless of his decision.

Lewis pondered for a minute, and then replied, "Son, if you have to eat a frog, don't stare at it too long before you start!"

As Sam had not told anyone about his dream, his father's statement was a confirmation to him that he should enlist. Sam had once heard that animals in your dreams represent your more primal instincts that are repressed in your waking life. He also took this as his father's approval for him to enlist. Sam then asked, "What will mother have to say?"

Lewis responded, "Before you tell anyone of your intentions, let me talk with her tonight. I need to prepare her for your decision."

The discourse that Lewis and Mary had that night included the realization that Sam was approaching the age where he could make his own decisions. They had always told their children that all choices they make have consequences, so make them wisely.

Chapter 6 – The Granville Rifles

It was June 11, 1861, three weeks after the train depot gathering in Henderson when Sam Reavis made the twelve mile trip from his home on Glebe Road to Kittrell in the southern part of the county. This is where Charles C. Blacknall, owner and operator of the Kittrell Springs Resort Hotel, was recruiting volunteers to enlist for one year in the Granville Rifles. This was the name selected for Company G, one of ten companies that would ultimately be a part of the North Carolina Twenty-Third Regiment. Initially formed as the 13th Regiment, the regiment would also be comprised of the Granville Stars and the Granville Ploughboys (later known as the Granville Targeteers), as well as seven companies from other counties.

Sam had been given a farewell sendoff by his family that morning. The event was encouraging as they were cheering him on. The exception was his mother Mary, who was quietly shedding tears. Many nights over the next four years, Sam would recall the scene of his family members on the front porch of the Reavis House as he descended the circular steps that day.

Upon Sam's arrival in Kittrell, he saw a number of his buddies and cousins. When he filled out his enlistment papers, he indicated that his age was 18. Sam was hoping that no one would question his age, as he was actually only 17. Sam rationalized that he was close enough to the required age to enlist, as his birthday was only five weeks off, on July 18. While other enlistees would get a $50 bounty for enlisting, Sam would not be eligible to get his bounty until he actually turned 18. In any event, Sam would be paid $11 per month for his service.

The hotel served as the training grounds for the Granville Rifles for several weeks. They remained in Kittrell until they joined other regimental companies at Weldon and Garysburg (in the northeastern part of the state) for another seven days of drilling. The volunteers, mostly farmers, underwent a little more drilling than they liked. But they realized that such tense drilling might possibly be necessary to whip Yankees and therefore submitted cheerfully. In addition to battle-related procedures, the men learned regulations regarding conduct and military life. They learned such things as how to address officers, how to store their knapsacks, and how to fold their clothing. They also learned how frequently they were to bathe (once per week), and how frequently they were to wash their feet (twice per week).

Wednesday, July 17, one day before Sam's eighteenth birthday, was an exciting day for Sam. Early that morning he and some 700 soldiers of the Twenty-Third boarded box cars of the Raleigh and Gaston Railroad. They had been told they were heading north to a train junction called Manassas,

Virginia. Anticipation was that they would likely be engaged in the first battle of the war, at a place called Bull Run. Not all members of the regiment could go because three of the ten companies came down with an outbreak of measles. Before boarding, each soldier was given a smooth bore percussion musket, paper cartridges containing powder, musket balls (bullets), and a bayonet. Upon being handed his musket and bayonet, the image of the frog named Alamo came to Sam's mind, as well as the dream of him fighting with Davy Crocket and Jim Bowie.

The next day, on Sam's birthday, the train was passing by several small-town stations that reminded him of the Henderson train depot. At one of the stations, Sam even saw a jack rabbit that reminded him of home. Enthusiasm was at a heightened level in a state of boundless hope. Cheers greeted Sam and the soldiers on every side as the train rolled by. It was a birthday Sam would always remember, and would later write home about.

It seemed as though they never would get to their destination. As things sometimes go wrong, the train trip was no exception. First, the train was traveling at less than normal speed for no known reason, prompting Captain Blacknall to accuse the engineer of treason. Second, the brakes got hot and one of the box cars full of gun powder caught fire. The box car had to be disconnected temporarily until it could cool.

Sunday, July 21 arrived and the train still had not reached Manassas. By way of telegraph, the train's passengers learned that the battle was already underway. This news made Sam and his buddies eager to get to their destination even more. One wonders if they knew to what extent their eagerness would wane in the months ahead, as the true grim aspects of war unfolded before them.

By late Sunday afternoon, the train had to be sidetracked at Louisa Court House, and again at Gordonville. The northbound train had to yield to the many southbound trains that bore wounded Confederates being taken to hospitals in Richmond. As the first train passed, Sam and his fellow soldiers stopped their cheering and horse play when they saw the cars of bloody-bandaged wounded. They later learned that nearly 400 Confederates had been killed and some 1,400 had been wounded at the First Battle of Bull Run.

Finally, shortly before midnight the train pulled into Manassas Junction. Perhaps by God's providence, the Twenty-Third had missed the battle completely. Sam said his prayers as he bedded down for the night on the hard box car floor made of pine boards. He could hear his stomach growling, as none of the men had eaten in the past twenty four hours. The last time they ate was when they were given rations in Richmond.

Monday morning arrived and as Sam looked through the cracks in his box car, he could tell that it was going to be a rainy, chilly, dismal day. What he saw as he departed the train horrified him. In some places around the station the mud must have been almost knee deep. The raindrops turned red as they fell onto the muddy ground, as there were rows of untended wounded who had lain in the field all night. Some of the wounded were horribly mutilated. The pile of amputated limbs outside an amputating tent seemed to continue to grow. Sam was reminded of the frog in his dream named Indian Trader and the two men whose ears had been disfigured.

The scene was an eye-opener to Sam, as well as to his fellow soldiers. Even the annual slaughtering of hogs back home could not have prepared him for the gory sights that day. This miserable day was the beginning of Sam's realization that war was not as glorious as he had envisioned. There's no telling what he would have done or how depressed he would have been if he only knew that such horrors would be commonplace over the next four years.

Private Samuel Wesley Reavis

Chapter 7 – Northern Virginia Fighting

The ten months following the Battle of Bull Run found the Twenty-Third joining regiments of other states performing outpost and picket duty. The Twenty-Third was more of a nomadic regiment, as the soldiers made their home at different encampments in Northern Virginia. The encampments included Camp Wigfall, Camp Ellis, Camp Mason Hills, and Camp Union Mills. They spent the winter in log huts that they built near Bull Run.

Sam did not mind being on picket. While there was danger, he did not have to engage in the type of fighting that took place at the First Battle of Bull Run. Actually, he was enjoying the hospitality of the citizens of Northern Virginia, who were appreciative of the protection they were being provided. The toughest part was the exposure to the hard winter, as after Christmas it either snowed or sleeted almost every day. While avoiding battle, a number of the men fell victim to death from pneumonia. This included two of the four Coghill brothers from Kittrell - James Norfleet and Joseph Wily.

A cousin of Sam, Asa C. Parham of Oxford, who had voluntarily enlisted with the Granville Rifles, became too weak to continue. Being 40 years of age, Asa was much older than most of the enlistees. Asa was discharged and allowed to go home for reason of "debility and heart." Still single at the time, shortly after he got back to Granville County he went to visit his Uncle Lewis and Aunt Mary Reavis. During the visit, he provided them an account of what the troops had experienced in Northern Virginia. He also assured them that Sam was holding up well as a soldier. He tried to convince them that an eighteen-year old could withstand much more than a forty-year old.

It would not be until the spring of 1862, ten months after leaving home, before the Granville Rifles saw any battle action. In March, the camp at Bull Run was abandoned, with migration back to Richmond for a brief period of time. In April, the regiment was sent to York Town, where they dug trenches. Sam was familiar with a pick and shovel, as he had used them extensively in clearing land back in Granville County. This was the first Easter that Sam had spent away from home. Although the troops were well dug-in, the order was given to abandon the trenches during the night of May 3 and retreat to Williamsburg, some twelve miles away. The Confederate spies had learned that Union General McClellan was planning a massive bombardment at dawn on May 5. When the time came for the attack, to the Yankee's surprise, the Confederates were long gone.

On the road to Williamsburg, there was an earthen Confederate fortification some 30 feet high, called Fort Magruder. It was on this road that Captain Blacknall and Private James Gill, who had gone out in advance of the regiment, encountered two Yankees hiding in the bushes. A Yankee bullet missed the Captain, but struck Private Gill, wounding him in the arm. Whipping out his sword, Blacknall overpowered the Yankees and took them as prisoners.

The historic town of Williamsburg was finally reached on May 5. The Confederates passed at double quick through the muddy streets. They were distressed at the shrieks of women and children who appeared terrified at the bloody drama that was going on before them. The soldiers made a short detour to the campus of William and Mary College to depose of all knapsacks and extra baggage. In later years, Sam would kiddingly tell others that he had gone to college there.

Shortly thereafter, the Battle of Williamsburg commenced, which took place in the pouring rain. The Twenty-Third was involved in a charge against the Yankees, but was forced to retreat back to the crest of a hill, where they held their ground until 3 o'clock in the morning. Again, under the cover of darkness, they made their escape, retreating back toward Richmond. While there were heavy losses at Williamsburg for the battalion, only five men of the Twenty-Third were wounded. This was the first bloodshed of the Granville Rifles. Sam was happy that he did not lose his boots, as some did when they were trudging through the mud mire that was knee deep at times. Sam only lost his knapsack, left behind at the campus of William and Mary.

Three weeks later, on May 31 and June 1, the Granville Rifles were engaged in the Battle of Seven Pines, a crossroads on the outskirts of Richmond. This was a critical battle in preventing the Yankees from laying siege to the Capital of the Confederacy. When the battle commenced, the Twenty-Third had to cross a swamp, thick with undergrowth and tangled vines and about waist deep in water. In addition to the Yankees, Sam was fearful of the snakes and wild hogs he encountered.

During the battle, Sam witnessed something that gave him a degree of courage that would carry him through the rest of the war. Captain Blacknall was on horseback and giving his men orders. Bullets kept coming at the Captain. Altogether, seven bullets grazed him, with a shell fragment hitting him in the back. Finally, his horse was shot out from under him, with a more serious injury to his leg as the horse fell on him. After the battle, Blacknall was promoted to Major, owing to Major Edmund Christian being killed. Sam was fortunate that he himself escaped harm, admiring the bravery demonstrated by his Captain.

After Seven Pines, the Twenty-Third went into camp near Richmond, where they drilled for several weeks. It was here that Sam for the first time saw General Robert E. Lee, who was now in charge of the Northern Army of Virginia. Just the sight of the General on his grey horse gave Sam chills as he rode by. Camped in tents upon a stream, the Twenty-Third had to be on high alert, as Union troops were lingering outside the city. This high alert rendered it necessary for the men to sleep with their cartridge belts on and knapsacks and canteens by their sides. Mounted officers had to keep their horses saddled, and no one was allowed to be absent from the command for any reason.

Over the remainder of June of 1862, there was a series of battles that was critical to protecting the City of Richmond. The first was the Battle of Mechanicsville, which began on June 26. The Twenty-Third was now under the command of General D.H. Hill. Early in the morning before the fighting started, Sam happened upon a group of what appeared to be high ranking Confederates talking under an oak tree. To Sam's surprise, he recognized four of them as President Jefferson Davis, General Lee, General Longstreet, and General Hill. From the men's overheard conversations, Sam deduced that an engagement was eminent.

Fighting at Mechanicsville Crossroads indeed did commence and lasted for two days. The fighting continued on at Cold Harbor. Colonel Christie, who had been wounded at the Battles of Seven Pines and Mechanicsville, was wounded for the third time at Cold Harbor, along Powhite Creek near Gaines Mill.

The last battle in the series of fighting, that would later be known collectively as the "Battle of Seven Days," was the Battle of Malvern Hill. Thus far, this was the bloodiest battle for the Twenty-Third. Sam had overheard Major Blacknall reporting to General Hill that 30 of his men had been killed, while 75 had been wounded. Upon seeing the three Union gunboats on the James River firing on the Confederates, Sam was reminded of the Frog named Blackbeard he had seen in his dream, and Blackbeard's ship, the *Queen Anne's Revenge*.

It was July 1862 and Sam had been in the Confederate Army for a whole year now. While he had only enlisted voluntarily for one year, the first Confederate Conscription Act prevented him from being able to go home. This was because the Act, which had just passed in April, extended his required service for another three years. Despite what he had been through over the past twelve months, Sam's spirits remained high, but he was becoming awfully homesick.

Chapter 8 – Brother Joins Brother

The first Confederate Conscription Act was enacted in April 1862. By this time, it was evident to President Jefferson Davis that an all-voluntary army would not be sufficient to win the war. The Confederate government apparently had overestimated its victory at the Battle of Bull Run, being confident that the war was won. The men who had volunteered a year earlier felt that the South wasted the summer and fall. By the time the Confederates prepared for action in the spring of 1862, the enlistments were running out, and the volunteers were eager to see home again. Even the more adventurous ones, like Private Sam Reavis, had seen all the glory they wanted to see. Upon learning of the passage of the Act, realization set in with Sam that he would not be returning home anytime soon.

Back in Granville County, while the Reavis Family on Glebe Road yearned for Sam's homecoming, the farm was doing fairly well without him. There were sufficient numbers of slaves to perform the planting and harvesting. (Lincoln's Emancipation Proclamation freeing the slaves in the South had not yet been issued.) However, the Conscription Act did mean that Lewis's son-in-law Alex Wortham, who was functioning as the farm's overseer, would likely be drafted soon.

The Conscription Act also raised concerns that Sam's older brother Thomas would not qualify for an exemption and would soon be drafted. Thomas, who was now 22 years old, was living with Bettie, his bride of two years. The notices went out, and a good number of men from Granville, Warren, and Franklin counties were constricted. For Thomas, his enlistment date was set for July 8. Needless to say, Thomas was not excited about having to enlist. One of the reasons was that in January his wife Bettie had given birth to their first child, Cora Tabitha.

Thomas, who now went by T.C. Reavis, elected to enroll with Company G of the Twenty-Third Regiment. This would enable him to be in the same company as his younger brother Sam. The Granville Rifles were in need of more enlistments, as a good number had been killed or wounded in the Seven Days Battle that took place between Williamsburg and Richmond.

On the early morning of July 8, 1862, T.C., along with his wife and daughter, went first to the Reavis House before leaving for duty later that day. Just as for Sam, the Reavis Clan gave T.C. a farewell celebration. On the top of the circular rock steps, T.C. gave a good-bye kiss to his mother Mary, wife Bettie, and six-month old Cora.

The sisters who were twins had turned 17 years old now. Not only were they sad about T.C. leaving, but they realized that their pickings of boyfriends would now be slim. Young John Billie and little sister Mary were looking forward to helping Bettie care for baby Cora while T.C. was gone. As T.C. passed the last of the cedar trees that lined the pathway heading toward Chalk Level, there to bid him farewell were a number of slaves and several beagles. A jack rabbit had also come out of hiding from the grapevines, seemingly to also bid him farewell. T.C. boarded the train in Henderson and headed north.

Sam was overjoyed when he saw T.C. disembark the train in Richmond. As one would expect, they gave each other a big bear hug. After the initial encounter, T.C. gave Sam a goodies bag that their mother had prepared for him. The most welcomed contents in the bag were fried apple jacks, which Sam had gone without for a year.

One week prior to T.C. arriving in Richmond, the Battle of Malvern Hill had ended. Union General McClellan had withdrawn his forces to assist in the fighting at Manassas and to safeguard the Federal Capital. This gave the Twenty-Third several weeks of grateful rest. While other troops continued to engage in battle, the Granville Rifles were held back and charged with protecting the City of Richmond. It was during this assignment in Richmond that T.C. and the other new enlistees joined the company.

Private T.C. Reavis had the opportunity to receive eight weeks of training before seeing any battle action. On September 2, the Twenty-Third was ordered to join the main Army of Northern Virginia at Chantilly, Virginia. This was three days after the Second Battle of Bull Run was over. It was also only one day after the Battle of Chantilly. Similar to Sam's experience after arriving at the First Battle of Bull Run a year earlier, T.C. got his first look at what the aftermath of battle looked like. The ground was covered with unburied dead. What was gruesome to T.C. were the many swollen corpses crushed and mangled by the cannon wheels, which in the urgency of that fierce and prolonged combat, had run over them.

After camping down in Chantilly for two days, the Twenty-Third joined in on the "Invasion of Maryland Campaign." On September 5, side-by-side, brothers T.C. and Sam waded with the Granville Rifles across the Potomac River at Noland's Ford. Maryland's residents were not as cordial as Virginia's residents had been, and many were not thrilled to see the Confederates going across their fields.

At one farm, General Hill, recognizing the hunger of his men, purchased an entire field of corn for his men to eat. The field of roasting corn reminded the Reavis brothers of the cornfields back home. There was even a jack rabbit in one of the cornfield rows that resembled the one T.C. had seen back home the day he left the Reavis House.

For several days the Twenty-Third remained in camp near Fredrick, Maryland. It was while at camp here that the infamous "lost note" was intercepted by a Union soldier. The note, wrapped around some Confederate cigars, contained valuable information regarding the Confederate's positions and Lee's military plans. This misfortune for the Confederacy, if acted upon appropriately by Union General McClellan, could have meant an early end to the Confederacy. McClellan even wrote to President Lincoln bragging that he would "catch them in their own trap."

McClellan did act upon the information obtained in the note. However, fortunately for the Confederates, McClellan's actions were not prompt enough and with sufficient force to overcome the counter actions of General Lee. The counter measures Lee took resulted in the Battle of South Mountain, where there was fighting over three different Blue Ridge Mountain passes.

It was Sunday, September 14 when Private T.C. Reavis was involved in his first skirmish. The Twenty-Third's position was in the center of Garland's Brigade and along the crest of a ridge above Fox Gap. The men of the Twenty-Third were stationed behind an old stone fence. The fence had been more or less dismantled by time and was very low in most places. Some 250 yards below the point where T.C. and Sam were both positioned, the NC Fifth Regiment faced off with the Federals in a cornfield. The fighting commenced at 9 o'clock that morning. Eventually, the main Confederate line had to retreat back up the hill to the stone fence where T.C. and Sam were entrenched. The Yankees, mostly Ohio troops, pressed forward up the steep hill, with many getting picked off as they advanced. All day, the Confederates warded off the repeated waves of attack, with losses being inflicted on both sides.

It was here that T.C. and Sam had their first experience fighting together against the enemy. While T.C. was the older brother, Sam was the veteran at fighting. Sam had always looked to T.C. for guidance growing up on the farm, but now the roles were reversed. With sufficient ammunition, from behind the stone wall T.C. and Sam kept shooting, reloading, and shooting their muskets. This was the first time either one had ever killed another human being. How many Yankees they killed that day, they did not know. They only knew they had to kill or be killed. Some say the heavy smoke from that battle is likely why today they call the range the Smoky Mountains.

When dusk came, it was evident that the Yankees' persistence was going to be successful. Word was received that Confederate General Samuel Garland had been killed. Seeing that capture was sure, Colonel Christie ordered the Twenty-Third to withdraw, which they did under the cover of darkness. The troops deployed to a gap near the Daniel Wise farm. It was only as the result of the timely arrival of reinforcements led by General Hood that kept the Twenty-Third from being wiped out completely.

T.C. and Sam later learned that the Yankees had dumped sixty Confederate bodies down Farmer Wise's well, paying the farmer compensation of $60.00. Disappointed of their perceived defeat at South Mountain, but proud of their courage, the Twenty-Third headed toward Sharpsburg. T.C. and Sam were just happy to have survived the fighting. Likewise, they were happy that neither of their bodies were among those thrown down the farmer's well.

Private Thomas Coghill Reavis

Chapter 9 – Bloody Wednesday

After fleeing South Mountain, the Confederates headed west toward the town of Sharpsburg. The Union Army pursued them, like a pack of hounds after rabbits. Many of the Confederates were barefooted and found it difficult to keep up in the march over the rough and stony road. Retreating in broad daylight along the Boonsboro Road, the Twenty-Third crossed the Middle Bridge over Antietam Creek. On the nights of September 15 and 16, they camped down in the fields southeast of the Roulette farm house. Sam Reavis and his older brother T.C. stuck close to each other, as the presence of the other gave them comfort and a sense of security.

When Sam and T.C. saw the Roulette farm house, they were struck by how much the two chimneys resembled those of the Reavis House back home. However, the steps of the Roulette House paled to the circular steps of the Reavis House. What was spooky to the brothers, were the buzzards they saw sitting on the chimneys, just like those sitting sometimes on the Reavis House. Such a sight frequently was an omen that death was soon to be experienced.

Early on the morning of the 17th, the Twenty-Third advanced across the Smoketown Road in support of Hood's Division. Sam and T.C. saw in the distance a vast cornfield that belonged to a Farmer Miller. By this time of the year, the corn stalks were turning brown, and their smell was one of the Reavis boys' favorite. The rustling of the stalk leaves and drooping tassels reminded them of the cornfields back home.

As they were advancing, the only threat initially was artillery fire coming from the opposite hill. Then all at once, the cornfield erupted into chaos as a fierce battle commenced. Men began beating each other over the heads with rifle butts and stabbing each other with bayonets. Sam and T.C. could see officers riding around on their horses yelling orders, but could not hear them over the noise of the battle. The Reavis boys' rifles became hot and dysfunctional from too much firing. The air around their heads was filled with bullets and artillery shells. Such fighting in the cornfield continued throughout the morning.

The following is an eyewitness account of Adjutant Vines E. Turner, a member of the Twenty-Third from Granville County, who later wrote of the encounter that next befell the regiment, around mid-morning:

"The brigade ....went into action with Colquitt's brigade in the Confederate center, and were advancing in perfect steadiness under a heavy artillery fire from the opposite hills, till the unaccountable 'run back' occurred. This happened as follows: The Federals advanced against us in dense lines through a corn field, which concealed the uniforms, though their flags and mounted officers could be seen plainly above the corn tassels. As the blue line became more distinct, approaching the edge of the corn field, which brought it in our range, we commenced to fire and effectively held it in check. But some of Early's men, who had come from the corn field, begged us not to fire, saying that their men were in our front. Someone in a regiment to the right of us also shouted: 'Cease firing! You are shooting your own men!' "

It was during this encounter in Miller's cornfield that Private T.C. Reavis felt a sharp sting in his left hand. At first he did not realize anything was wrong, as he was more concerned about avoiding bullets that were whizzing by his head. However, several minutes later he noticed something red on his coat sleeve. He thought to himself, "It could not be." But then he realized that he had been shot. "Sam!" T.C. hollered out, "I've been hit!" It was unclear if T.C. had been hit by enemy fire or if it was the result of friendly fire, although official records would later record that he had been "wounded accidently."

Being both confused and threatened, the men in the front of the skirmish halted and began retreating, prompting a mass "run back" of the entire regiment. T.C.'s realization that he had been injured made him feel as though he was going to pass out. Noticing how white T.C's complexion was, Sam grabbed his older brother by the arm that was not injured and led him in the direction of the retreat. They went south pass Dunker Church and then headed east down "Sunken Road," which would later be known as "Bloody Lane."

The road, worn down by years of wagon traffic, provided the Confederates a strong defensive position, as it was atop a gradual ridge and formed a natural trench. The Confederates occupied a stretch of road for about eight hundred yards. For over three hours, in the heat of the day, Union troops repeatedly made attacks against the Confederates positioned along the Sunken Road. With nowhere else to go, Sam and T.C. dug in at a spot on the western end of the road. They picked a spot that allowed them to avoid being in the line of fire. Sam removed the scarf from a dead soldier lying in the trench and wrapped it around T.C.'s wrist to control the bleeding. He also removed the dead soldier's belt to make a sling for T.C. After getting settled down, Sam offered up a prayer on the dead soldier's behalf.

For a period of time, the Confederates in the trench seemed to withstand the barrage of enemy bullets. However, a breach occurred in the center of the line of defense. This gave the Yankees a tactical opportunity to fire directly into the Sunken Road from a different angle, with the Confederates now being like sitting ducks.

It was at this point that T.C. was wounded a second time. An enemy bullet pierced his right leg, with the bullet going completely through. When the bullet hit him this time, he knew it immediately. T.C. yelled out, "Heavens to Betsy!"

Sam was not sure if T.C. was calling out to his wife Bettie back home or not. Just as he had cared for his brother earlier, Sam again requisitioned a belt and scarf from a fallen comrade. Sam used them to make a tourniquet and bandage for the bleeding wound. The pain reminded T.C. of the time he had injured his leg as a lad when he slipped and fell on ice one night on the circular rock steps back home.

In late afternoon the main fighting shifted to the southern part of Sharpsburg. Sam and T.C. saw this as an opportunity to leave the Sunken Road and attempt to regroup with the rest of the Twenty-Third. However, T.C.'s level of anxiety was increasing. Being trapped for several hours, he was fearful he would succumb to his injuries. With a shivering voice, T.C. told his brother, "Sam, you may have to leave me here. There's no way you can carry my weight."

With a tear showing, Sam responded, "T.C. there's no way I'm leaving you here to die. Mother would never forgive me." He then added, "Remember what father's watch says. 'This too shall pass!' "

Indeed, Sam would have a difficult time bearing his brother's weight, considering the distance they had to cover. Fortunately, as if an answer to prayer, Private James Stone of Kittrell saw the Reavis brothers and offered to assist them.

The three men struggled for over a mile before reaching the regimental camp. Along the way, as the sun was going down in the west, they often had to step over dead and wounded soldiers, both Confederates and Yankees. Amongst the smoke filled air and blood stained ground, many of the wounded were calling out for help. It was disheartening to the three men that they were unable to help those crying out in pain.

After finally reaching camp, T.C. was seen briefly by the regimental surgeon, Doctor Robert Hicks. However, there were many more seriously wounded than T.C., and he had to rely upon Sam to tend to his bandages. T.C. was just grateful that his hand or leg did not have to be amputated like many others.

The Twenty-Third bedded down that night, being on watch for another possible attack. The next day, after seeing the devastation of the killed and wounded, both sides were too feeble and depressed to continue fighting. Attention was finally given to tending to the wounded. Confederate reinforcements had arrived from Harpers Ferry, which also prevented the Union forces from attacking again. Orders were given for Lee's Army to cross the Potomac River near Shepherdstown and head back to Virginia.

The Battle of Sharpsburg, which the Northerners referred to as the Battle of Antietam, would later be referred to as "Bloody Wednesday," with over 22,000 soldiers being either killed or wounded. The sights and sounds witnessed by the two Reavis brothers that day would haunt them for the rest of their lives, and T.C. would bear the battle scars as both proof and a reminder.

Chapter 10 – Brothers Separated

After leaving Sharpsburg, the Twenty-Third headed back to Virginia. However, the time had come for Sam and T.C. to be separated due to the injuries T.C. had received in battle. Sam stayed with the regiment, which encamped along Opequon Creek in the western part of Virginia. T.C. on the other hand was transported along with the other wounded to a hospital in Richmond. It had been only two and one-half months that the two brothers were together. However, due to the extensive battles they fought in together, it seemed like a lifetime.

While at the Opequon Creek camp, Sam and the Twenty-Third would have five weeks to rest and recuperate from the Battle of Sharpsburg. T.C. on the other hand was admitted to the Richmond General Receiving Hospital located on Grace Street where he received attention to his two wounds. The injury to the right leg was a clean wound, as the bullet had passed straight through without touching any bones. The injury to the left hand and wrist however was more serious, as there were multiple bone fractures. Also, infection had set in causing a redness to extend up the entire arm. There were several discussions about the possibility of amputating his left arm below the elbow. T.C. adamantly objected to this option.

While soldiers feared the bullet as a killer, nearly half of all war deaths resulted, not from injuries, but from some type of infectious disease. For weeks, T.C. had a very high fever, often experiencing chills and shaking. This precarious condition existed through Christmas of 1862 and well into the next year.

At the end of January, T.C. was transferred to General Hospital Number 24, the hospital designated primarily for soldiers from the State of North Carolina. The hospital, also more commonly referred to as Moore Hospital, was a converted tobacco factory. Having a capacity of 120 patients, it was a three-story brick building located on the corner of Main Street and 26th Street. Just that month, the "Ladies of Island Creek" in Granville County had sent a donation of $50 to the hospital, for the benefit of the men from the Carolinas.

T.C. remained at Moore Hospital for only a short period of time before being transferred to a third hospital. On February 17 he was transferred to Chimborazo Hospital, a convalescent hospital located on the eastern edge of Richmond. He was treated at this hospital for another two months. It was here that T.C. celebrated his 23rd birthday on March 20. One of the male Negro nurses, a former slave, baked and brought him a cake from his home.

During T.C.'s stay at each of the three hospitals, he was able to write home to his parents and his wife Bettie. He also received letters from back home, keeping him abreast of all happenings. Bettie wrote of how much she missed him on their second wedding anniversary on December 10, which was a lonely time for her. She also reminded him of two birthdays he had missed: her own 19th birthday on December 18th, and their daughter Cora's first birthday on January 25. Bettie also informed him that Cora was now walking. Although he missed spending these important dates with his family while hospitalized, he was happy to be alive, and to once again be walking himself.

As new wounded soldiers were admitted to whatever hospital T.C. may be in at the time, he would learn of the battles that he was missing. He was particularly interested in the happenings of the Twenty-Third, as the welfare of his brother Sam was always on his mind. He was also interested in the happenings of the Fifty-Fourth Regiment, the regiment to which his brother-in-law Alex Wortham belonged. Alex had enlisted a year earlier in April 1862. Little did T.C. know that Alex, who had married his older sister Lucy, would be admitted to a Richmond Hospital, just days after T.C. would be released.

Once a soldier was admitted to a hospital, there is one of several ways he could leave. He could be returned to duty, be discharged, be furloughed, or be transferred. Alternately, he could either desert or die. T.C. witnessed all of these events, with more dying than he preferred to see. In T.C.'s case, on April 3, 1863 he was fortunate enough to be granted a sick furlough. Altogether, he had spent six months in three different Richmond hospitals. The 30-day furlough allowed him to return home for further recuperation, before having to report for duty. The good news was, when he returned for duty he would be detailed to Raleigh, North Carolina to serve as a provost guard. This meant he would only be forty-five miles from his home.

Before leaving the hospital, T.C. bade farewell to the surgeons and nurses that had tended him. He expressed his gratitude for nursing him through his injuries and infectious disease. T.C. wasted no time making arrangements to board a southbound train at the Richmond depot. The train passed through the same towns that he had passed through the previous July when he traveled north. At each stop along the way, he noticed that there seemed to be a gloom hanging over the citizens, almost like a dark cloud.

The train was scheduled to reach the train depot in Henderson around 5 o'clock that afternoon. Being on schedule, the train passed through Chalk Level, which was less than fifteen minutes away from Henderson. Although Chalk Level was two miles south of the Reavis House, the train whistle could clearly be heard by the animals on the farm that day. Two beagle dogs sitting on the top of the circular rock steps began to howl, as if they knew that T.C. was on the train they could hear in the distance.

Waiting at the train depot to welcome T.C. home was the entire Reavis household. It was the moment the Reavis Clan had been anxiously awaiting ever since they received word a week earlier that T.C. was being furloughed. It was not a grand homecoming attended by large numbers of townsfolk, as T.C. was the only soldier that was getting off of the train that day. As the train came to a halt, the screech of the brakes could be heard, and the dark smoke from the engine filled the station area.

The most anxious among those waiting was wife Bettie, who was now nineteen years old. Bettie was a petite young lady with long dark brown hair, which was parted in the middle, then pulled back, forming a neatly tight bun. Bettie wore the same dress she adorned when they got married almost two and one-half years earlier. It was a light grey cotton dress, with black horizontal stripes extending across the top front, accented with a white laced collar that fit gracefully around her neck. She also wore the teardrop cross necklace that T.C. had given her when they courted.

As Bettie saw T.C. dimly through the train's window, all of the romantic yearnings she had kept penned up swept across her mind. For too many lonely nights she had laid in bed alone, wondering if her soul mate was safe or not, and if he would ever come home. She had missed dearly the tender romantic times they had shared together. Now, as she saw him through the train window, she could almost smell his fragrance and feel his whiskers on the back of her neck from the hug she was about to receive.

As T.C. stepped down from the train, holding the rail with his uninjured right hand, the whole Reavis Clan shouted out in unison, "Hurray for T.C.!" Bettie ran to meet him and gave him the hug she had been dreaming of ever since he left. His mother Mary was holding baby Cora, who were each next to receive hugs. The rest of the family stood in line awaiting their turn. This included his father Lewis, the twin girls Della and Ella, younger sister Mary, younger brother John Billie, older sister Martha and her husband John, and sister Lucy. It was then that they all noticed how weak and pale T.C. looked. Being six foot tall, he must have weighed no more than 160 pounds, some 40 pounds less than the last time they had seen him.

They all climbed onto the three wagons they had arrived in. T.C. had to be helped up onto one of the wagons by his father. All aboard, the family headed back to the Reavis

House. They passed through Chalk Level and turned down Glebe Road, with T.C.'s wagon leading the way. The caravan passed several neighboring families along the roadside, including the Worthams and the Baskets who were waiting to greet T.C. as he rode by.

As they turned onto the path lined with the cedar trees that led up to the Reavis House, the first thing that T.C. saw was a jack rabbit hiding in the grapevines. Next, looking up the hill, he saw the three chimneys, the boxwood bushes, the covered well, and the circular steps. He knew then that he was home.

Although the family first led him to the back door, where there were fewer steps to climb, T.C. insisted that he wanted to go around front and go up the rock steps into the house. This he did, with Bettie's assistance. And when T.C. got to the top step with the petrified water vein running through it, he paused, bowed his head and said a silent prayer.

Bettie Best Reavis

Chapter 11 – Wolf by the Ear

During the period of time Private T.C. Reavis was in the hospital in Richmond, his brother Sam was encamped on Opequon Creek in western Virginia, and his brother-in-law Alex was encamped on the Rappahannock River in Virginia. Also during this time, Lincoln's Proclamation of Emancipation was issued. The Proclamation, which took effect January 1, 1863, freed all slaves in the states that were in rebellion, but not in the states or territories that remained a part of the Union.

While there were some slave owners in the South, as well as in the North, who adamantly opposed the absolution of slavery, there was a growing number who morally knew it was wrong. This latter view was taken largely by men of faith, who were in hopes that the spread of Christianity would eventually be the catalyst that ended the institution of slavery, instead of a bloody conflict.

Lewis Reavis had views similar to those of Robert E. Lee and Thomas Jefferson. Lewis had frequently quoted Lee, "There are few, I believe, in this enlightened age, who will not acknowledge that slavery as an institution is a moral and political evil....How long their servitude may be necessary is known and ordered by a merciful Providence. Their emancipation will sooner result from the mild and melting influences of Christianity than from the storm and tempest of fiery controversy."

Thomas Jefferson, an owner of thirteen slaves himself, abhorred slavery. Years earlier he had predicted the eventual demise of the evil, likely as a result of a bloody process. However, Jefferson recognized the "ancestral burden" that had been placed upon all slave owners.

Jefferson had been quoted as saying, "Until that presumably distant day, however, it was the duty of every slaveholding gentleman to shoulder the ancestral burden as best he could, for the good of both races: there was no place for free blacks in a slave-based society." In a letter to John Holmes in 1820, Jefferson expressed himself this way, "We have the wolf by the ear, and we can neither hold him, nor safely let him go."

Lewis Reavis now knew that Lee's hope of a Christian-influenced solution was not in the cards. He also knew that the time had come for Jefferson's "wolf by the ear" to be let go. However, Lewis was relieved that the "ancestral burden" that had been placed upon him by his father was now being lifted from him. The breaking of the generational chain would relieve his descendants of having to carry this ancestral burden as well. But most of all, he was delighted that the inherent and unalienable rights of man were now being bestowed upon the slaves, whose livelihood had been entrusted to the Reavis Family.

One dark chapter in the Reavis Family pertained to a portion of the 34 slaves that were inherited by the children of Samuel Jones Reavis upon his death nine years earlier in 1854. Acting as co-administrators of their father's estate, the sons Lewis and Thomas posted a $60,000 bond with the Granville County Clerk of Court. On the same day, they had a jury declare their younger brother, Richard R. Reavis, a "lunatic." Thomas was appointed Richard's guardian.

While Thomas took good care of Richard, Thomas took advantage of his power and control over Richard's inherited slaves. Thomas was accused of inappropriately charging rent to Richard for caring for his slaves. This abuse of power did not go unpunished, as the Granville Clerk of Court would later sue Thomas for the mishandling of Richard's guardianship. Lewis discovered that family members do not always do the right thing. Because Lewis looked out for the interest of mentally-challenged Richard and his slaves, Lewis earned the respect of many slaves in the community.

During the days leading up to the freedom date of January 1, 1863, there was more singing in the Reavis slave quarters than usual. The singing of gospel songs could be heard well after midnight. Having obtained a copy of the Proclamation, Lewis Reavis gathered his 17 slaves together on New Year's Day for the purpose of reading the document to them. Lewis wanted to do this as opposed to the slaves hearing it from a Federal officer. Being a mild winter day, Lewis decided that he would address the slaves from atop the circular rock steps, a platform that would allow all to see and hear him. These were the same steps that the ancestors of some of those gathered had labored to build seventy-two years earlier, before any of them had been born.

All the slaves gathered at the bottom of the steps, bundled together to keep warm and curious as to what their Master was about to tell them. There were five adult men (the oldest being 70 years old), six adult females (the oldest being 48 years old), and six children (four-to-five years old). The only other thing stirring was a jack rabbit that was seen hiding in the boxwood bushes.

Having heard through the grapevine of the Proclamation, the slaves assumed the gathering was about the document. Lewis greeted them first and expressed his hopes that they had a Merry Christmas. He then read to them the Proclamation, in its entirety. Recognizing that some of the listeners did not comprehend what the legalistic words meant, Lewis proceeded to explain the meaning to them. He told them the bottom line was that they were now all free, and could go when and where they pleased.

Lewis wanted the tone of his delivery to be one of acceptance, and for the listeners to recognize the sincerity of his message. He did not want them to get the impression, like some planters were giving, that he was going to ignore the Proclamation. In his message, he shared with them his views on the institution of slavery. Second, he wanted to celebrate with them their Day of Jubilation, which had been long coming. Lewis alluded to the Providence of God, which he knew they could comprehend, since the slaves were all serious about their religious beliefs.

However, from a practical standpoint, Lewis knew that the Proclamation would cause serious problems, not only as it related to the continued operation of the farm, but for the welfare of the freed slaves as they transitioned to free people. Not only were Lewis's two older sons off at war, but his overseer Alex Wortham was as well. This situation posed a real problem for Lewis should the slaves abandon him. Additionally, Lewis felt he had an obligation to the continued welfare of the freed slaves that had been entrusted to him until they arrived at the point where they could truly be independent and self-sufficient.

To address the problems, Lewis offered the freed slaves the opportunity to stay on the farm and work under a contract arrangement. He also indicated that he would be open to sharecropper arrangements. Under such arrangement, the tenant would work the land for an agreed share of the crop proceeds, with deductions for living quarters and food provided to the tenant. Lewis told them however, that should they chose to leave, they could not come back. He had a good idea which ones were likely to flee for good. Regardless of their eventual choice, Lewis knew that the value of his estate just plummeted nearly $18,000, as these human beings were no longer considered his personal property.

When Lewis finished his address, the immediate reaction was by Patience, the house slave. Looking up toward heaven, she began to cry with tears of joy. The one prayer request she had been lifting up for years was now being answered. Being speechless, the only thing she could do was to hug her little boy standing beside her. The next reaction was from Baldy, the strongest of the Negro men, to whom all others looked to as a leader. Baldy hollered at the top of his voice, "Jubilee! Jubilee!" The rest of the adult Negros joined in and repeated the cheer.

As the freed slaves went back to their quarters, Lewis watched the several children who were less than six years old. He wondered to himself if they would remember this day once they grew up as free people.

Chapter 12 – Too Sick to Fight

Three months prior to T.C. Reavis being drafted into the Confederate Army in July 1862, Alex Wortham, the husband of his sister Lucy Reavis, elected to voluntarily enlist. While T.C. would later enlist with the Twenty-Third Regiment to be with his younger brother Sam, Alex opted for another regiment. He chose to enlist with the newly formed Fifty-Fourth Regiment, Company K. Alex's choice of regiments was primarily because he knew the Captain of Company K, Samuel Jones Parham. Captain Parham was his wife's first cousin, as his mother was Delia Hawkins Reavis, sister to Lewis Pleasant Reavis. In fact, Delia and her husband Asa Parham had four sons altogether who served in the Confederate Army.

Just like for Alex's two brothers-in-law, the Reavis Clan gave Alex a send-off from the Reavis House. The family gathered for breakfast that cool April morning. The ladies cooked Alex's favorites – scrambled eggs, grits with red-eye gravy, and topped off with molasses biscuits. All seemed upbeat about Alex going off to fight for the cause, all that is except for his wife Lucy. A year into the war now, Lucy had heard about the various battles. She was aware of other ladies in the county whose husbands had gone off to fight and were either wounded, captured, or killed. Lucy was torn between two attitudes to demonstrate that day – show her support for the cause that Alex was going to fight for, or levy a guilt trip on Alex for leaving. She was unusually quiet that morning during breakfast. However, when it came time for Alex to leave, she decided to take control of her emotions and give Alex her blessing. She knew that he would have a better chance of survival if he knew he had a supportive wife waiting for him to return home.

Attending the send-off that morning were Alex's parents, Billy and Fanny Wortham. William "Billy" Duke Wortham was an ardent supporter of the war, and his enthusiasm of Alex's enlistment was evident. Fanny's attitude on the other hand was more in line with that of Lucy.

As Alex commenced his departure by descending the circular steps, the entire family congregated on the front porch and steps to bid him farewell. During the months ahead, Alex would have memories of Lucy escorting him down the steps that morning and giving him a hug and kiss he would never forget. Except for a lingering cold, Alex felt good as he left the house and headed toward Chalk Level where he would meet up with other enlistees heading to camp. Lewis and Mary both put their arms around Lucy as tears were starting to fall down her cheeks.

Alex and the other enlistees met up with Captain Parham in Henderson. The company of men then headed to drill camp located at Camp Campbell near Kinston. Alex enjoyed being with the other enlistees and did not mind the drilling at all. It was looking as if soldiering was easier than farming, although his lingering cold seemed to drain the strength out of him. Alex appeared to be a strong healthy man, standing at six feet two inches tall. However, after two months of ardent drilling, his cold progressed to the point where he was having problems breathing. Then one afternoon after drilling in the hot July sun, Alex felt as if a monkey was on his back and collapsed.

For several weeks, Alex was attended to in the regiment's sick tent by the doctor. Then it came time for the regiment to head north to join Lee's Army. The doctor determined that Alex was too ill to travel with the regiment and granted him a sick furlough to return home to recover. No one was happier to see Alex return home than Lucy.

For three months Lucy nursed Alex until orders were received for him to return to the regiment, which was now encamped in Northern Virginia. It was an autumn day, with leaves turning vibrant hues of orange and yellow when the family was to take Alex to the train station in Henderson and once again send him on his way. Alex descended the rock steps and walked across the front yard past the black walnut tree. Stepping on the many walnuts lying on the ground, he hoped that this would not be the last time he felt the walnuts beneath his feet.

Apparently, Alex had not fully recovered from his illness. The resumption of drilling in the cool damp November air was enough to send him to the regimental sick tent again. On December 6, the regimental doctor admitted Alex to Moore Hospital in Richmond for treatment of pleurisy. This was just one week before the Battle of Fredericksburg, the first battle in which the Fifty-Fourth Regiment would be engaged. Somewhat eager to fight, Alex's frail health condition would prevent him from doing so at this time, perhaps for his own good.

Hospitalized at Moore Hospital with Alex was Private Josiah Parham, a member of the Granville Grays, Company D of the NC Twelfth Regiment. Josiah, who had pneumonia, was a cousin of Alex's wife Lucy. Alex and Josiah talked about the good old days back home. They also talked about their faith, as Alex was a member of Geneva Presbyterian Church, and Josiah was a devoted member of nearby Salem Methodist Church.

On Christmas Day, they were both well enough to eat dinner together and were able to celebrate the occasion. However, two days later, Josiah's condition became grave and he asked the nurse to summon Alex. Alex came to his bedside and for the last three hours of Josiah's life, Alex prayed with him. Josiah's last request was for Alex to tell his parents, Mary Tatum Hicks and Lewis Reavis Parham that he loved them dearly. Unlike many patients in the hospital who died alone, Josiah passed peacefully being comforted by a fellow believer.

After Christmas, for a second time Alex was furloughed home for recuperation. Lewis, Mary, and Lucy met him at the train station in Henderson and took him home where Lucy once more nursed him. Being not far from the overseer house where Alex and Lucy lived, Mary Reavis assisted them nearly every day. Alex remained on furlough this time for two months, somewhat thankful that he did not have to endure the cold weather months on a battlefield somewhere. No one was any happier than Lucy for Alex to be home on furlough to keep her warm that winter.

Orders were received in mid-February 1863 for Alex to return to the regiment before the first of March. It was during their last night together that Alex and Lucy's love overflowed to the point that a baby was conceived. When Alex departed the next day to return to duty, no one but the Lord was aware that Lucy was with child. Somehow, Lucy knew that she may never see Alex again. Little did they know that this last night together would result in their only daughter being born, from whom there would be many Reavis descendants.

Upon Alex's return to duty in March, the Regiment was now encamped on the Rappahannock River. The cold rainy weather was not conducive to Alex, as on April 18 he was once again hospitalized at Moore Hospital in Richmond with pneumonia. On May 8, he was transferred to Hospital Number 21 located at the corner of 25th and Cary Street for further treatment. As Alex was hospitalized recuperating from pneumonia, he was also diagnosed as having rheumatism, which explained his severe joint problems.

As Alex lay in the hospital bed for a month, he experienced many emotions. He felt guilty that he was not able to fight and was concerned that his fellow soldiers were viewing him as a coward trying to dodge the fighting. He also felt guilty that he was not home helping to run the Reavis farm. Most of all, he was missing being at home with Lucy who was now expecting their first child. The thoughts of becoming a father was one thing that kept his spirits up.

With the Confederates desperately needing troops, on May 14, 1863, Alex was returned to duty, even though he was still weak. As fate would have it, as a result of being hospitalized for the third time, Alex had missed the Battle of Chancellorsville. This was the battle in which Confederate

Lieutenant General Stonewall Jackson was killed. Alex rejoined his regiment as it headed toward the Shenandoah Valley. This was a "first" for Alex, as he had never seen the mountains before.

It had been a full year since Alex enlisted, and he had yet to experience any battle fighting. However, things were about to change. Now a part of Early's Division under General Ewell, in June the Fifty-Fourth Regiment headed into the Blue Ridge Mountains of Virginia. It was here that the regiment would be engaged in the Second Battle of Winchester.

It was on the outskirts of Kernstown that Alex was involved in his first skirmish. Needless to say, Alex was scared and his fear was showing. Recognizing Alex's fear, Captain Parham took him to the side and told him: "Son, when faced with fear, you can either be intimidated or be motivated. I expect you to be motivated today!" These were the words a scared soldier needed to hear.

The skirmish started around noon and lasted for a solid four hours, with the Confederates eventually pushing the Union troops back. Alex had survived his first battle and was elated that the Confederates decisively defeated the Yankees that day. He was proud that he had faced his fear. But he also knew he was fortunate to escape without injury and with his life intact.

On June 16, Alex's regiment, then numbering 400 men, was ordered to escort 2,000 Union prisoners captured at Winchester to Staunton, a distance of 100 miles. From Staunton, they then escorted the prisoners via train to Richmond. Marching eighteen miles a day and guarding prisoners at night, the regiment accomplished its assignment and returned to Winchester on July 3. Under the command of Colonel Murchison, the regiment was next ordered by General George Imboden to guard an ordnance wagon train heading to Williamsport, Pennsylvania. This was the town in which the Underground Railroad, an organization to assist escaped slaves had been organized.

Fortunately for Alex, these guard assignments for the Fifty-Fourth Regiment spared him from having to experience the Battle of Gettysburg, another "close miss" for Alex. However, on July 5 and 6, Alex saw the aftermath of that great battle, as Williamsport became a general hospital for the many wounded arriving there by train. Never in his life would Alex witness such suffering among the wounded as he had those two days.

Alex then experienced his second battle skirmish on July 6. The regiment successfully held off a fierce one-hour attack on the wagon train, with the fighting starting about 5 o'clock in the afternoon. During the attack, Union troops advanced their artillery, which was followed by dismounted cavalry. Once the Union troops retreated, Alex was fortunate not to be one of the twenty-five regimental men who were either wounded or killed that day.

On July 8, at Hagerstown, Maryland, the Fifty-Fourth Regiment then joined up with the main Army that had retreated from Gettysburg. For the first time since the war started, Alex Wortham would be in the same vicinity as his brother-in-law Sam Reavis, who arrived there on July 6 to fight in what was to be known as the Battle of Hagerstown. Alex was hopeful that their paths would cross.

Chapter 13 – Home Front

It was the end of June of 1863. Lewis and Mary Reavis of Granville County now had two sons and a son-in-law enlisted in the Confederate Army, not to mention about a dozen of their nephews. The oldest son T.C. had come home on a sick furlough, having spent six months in three different Richmond hospitals for treatment of wounds incurred at the Battle of Sharpsburg. The younger son Sam was with the Twenty-Third Regiment somewhere north of Virginia. The husband of their daughter Lucy, Alex Wortham, was fighting with the Fifty-Fourth Regiment in Williamsport, Pennsylvania. Alex had only just recently been released from a hospital in Richmond due to pneumonia, which had followed a bout with pleurisy.

Times at home were getting tough. As a result of Lincoln's Proclamation of Emancipation in January of that year, some of the slaves had abandoned Lewis and Mary Reavis, seeking better opportunities with other planters or public work. However, a core of the slaves stayed on and entered into sharecropper arrangements. Economically, things were not going well, as most North Carolinians were feeling the effects of the Union blockade. Goods such as leather shoes, coffee, salt, and factory-made cloths were no longer readily available. Prices of staples had sky-rocketed, with inflation becoming a major enemy. A barrel of flour that normally sold for eighteen dollars in 1862 was now selling for thirty-five dollars.

Lewis Reavis was able to capitalize on the high prices of staples. The 1st NC Calvary Regiment had established Camp Beauregard some ten miles away in Ridgeway. The regiment's Quartermaster made frequent purchases of supplies from Lewis during 1863, just when the Reavis Family needed money the most. On May 14, the Quartermaster purchased 624 pounds of bacon at a dollar per pound, for a total price of $624.00. Other sales during the year included blade fodder for the horses and posts for fencing.

T.C.'s wife Bettie was busy taking care of Cora, who was three years old now. Alex's wife Lucy was six-months pregnant and was showing greatly. The twin girls, Della and Ella, were eighteen years old and were somewhat dejected that there were no boys around for any romance. John Billie was a teenager, and young Mary was almost a teenager. All of these children were being called upon to do more chores. While the former house slave was providing some servant type services, she was now free to stay in her own quarters at night. Previously, house slaves had slept in the basement of the house.

When the war started, the oldest daughter Martha Vaughan had two children, Nora and Belle. Now Martha and her husband John Vaughan had three children, with a son having been born in March of 1863.

Mary knew that the men off at war were fighting not only for their property and liberty, but for their mothers, wives, and sisters. Accordingly, although she had great concern for the fighting men, in all of her letters to them she conveyed a deep sense of strength. Conversely, she was very apprehensive and prayed continuously for their safety, health, and return. Mary's husband Lewis was a strong one, both physically and spiritually. He kept the farm going and made sure that the family kept up their church attendance and scripture reading. What was taxing on him though were the occasional feelings of depression stemming from the family's financial struggles. However, he was strengthened each time he read the engraving on his timepiece - "This too shall pass!"

While Private T.C. Reavis was doing well physically since he had arrived home the first week of April, mentally he was not. He was having difficulty sleeping, often waking up at night with nightmares stemming from the sights and horrors he experienced during battle. The images of the pleading men he saw when he was helped off the battlefield at Sharpsburg weighed heavy on his mind. Whenever a thunderstorm came up, the family noticed that he would jump at the sound of thunder. Such behavior was characteristic of soldiers who had been exposed to cannonades. Bettie observed that T.C. would easily get agitated with her over the smallest thing.

While T.C. had come home on furlough the first week of April, he was withholding some important information from his family, including Bettie. The family's assumption was that the furlough was for as long as needed for his full recovery. Apparently, T.C. was in a state of denial and maybe had even convinced himself that he did not have to return to duty. He also rationalized that the family needed his labor to work the crops, as the slaves had been freed in January. It was not unheard of for soldiers to take temporary leave to go home during crop planting time.

Thus far, even though T.C. had now been "absent without leave" for two months, there did not seem to be any consequences of his overstay of leave. While T.C. in his mind did not consider himself to be a deserter, he still had an uneasy feeling about not returning to duty. He felt guilty whenever the family received letters from either Sam or Alex describing their episodes. T.C. knew of other soldiers who had overstayed their leave and were punished by being assigned fatigue duty. In some cases they were sentenced to grubbing stumps, and in some cases assigned double guard duty.

It was July 4th when T.C. happened to be the one who went to the Post Office in Henderson to get the family's mail, a trip that was made at least once per week. The Confederate Post Mistress was Elizabeth Reavis, T.C's first cousin. Elizabeth was the 43-year old spinster daughter of William Whitfield Reavis, who had been the U.S. Postmaster before his death in 1861. Elizabeth considered herself a devoted Confederate and had no use whatsoever for Yankees. In fact, when the war would eventually end, she would refuse to take the Oath of Allegiance. Taking the oath was a requirement to hold any type of government job. Elizabeth would be forced to relinquish the position to her younger sister Sarah, who was not as much a construed Rebel. Elizabeth died in 1894 at the age of 78 after being stung by a swarm of hornets, due to her pouring hot water on the nest. Even then, she resented the Carpetbaggers who had invaded the South.

When Elizabeth saw her cousin T.C. at the mail pickup window, she greeted him as normal, but this time showed an aura of curiosity. This was because she had an envelope addressed to him, with the return address, "Under Secretary of War, Confederate States of America." Elizabeth seemed to know everyone's business, having the opportunity to see what type of correspondence the county's citizens received. She was a source of information when it came to knowing the fate of the county's soldiers. Elizabeth had been wondering why T.C. was still on sick furlough and not off at war like his brother Sam and his brother-in-law Alex.

When T.C. was handed the envelope, he felt a lump in his throat, as he had a pretty good idea what it contained. T.C. took the envelope without as much as acknowledging Elizabeth. He quickly tucked the envelope in his coat pocket, got back onto his horse and sped away toward home. As T.C. rode down Glebe Road, he thought about stopping to open the envelope. However, either he was too scared to open it, or just did not want to know what was in it.

When T.C. got to the Reavis House, he saw his wife Bettie and daughter Cora sitting on the bottom row of the circular rock steps. Cora started jumping for joy when she saw her daddy. T.C. rode around to the covered well, dismounted, and tied the horse to the hitching post. He then went around to the steps where his family was sitting. Bettie could tell that something was bothering her husband as he approached.

T.C. sat down beside his wife, and without saying a word, carefully opened the envelope with his pocket knife. After removing and unfolding the letter, he read it out loud, "Special Order to Private Thomas Coghill Reavis, NC Twenty-Third Regiment. You are hereby ordered to report to duty no later than July 8, 1863 at Camp Holmes in Raleigh, Wake County, being detailed as a provost guard. This detail away from the Twenty-Third Regiment is due to your wounds incurred in service. Failure to report to this detail will result in a charge of desertion." The letter was signed by the Under Secretary of War, Confederate States of America.

T.C. felt a sigh of relief. In a way he was glad the letter had finally come. He knew it could be worse, as he could have been cited for being a deserter. He looked at Bettie, who did not seem surprised, as she had suspected all along that T.C. had overstayed his furlough. T.C. and Bettie would have four more nights together before he made the 45-mile trip to Raleigh. Signs of T.C.'s healing were good sights for Bettie to see and experience. Bettie knew the war was nowhere near its end and that T.C. needed to be mentally strong to endure whatever he had to face being a provost guard. Understanding the power of a woman, she remembered what her mother had once told her: "A man is only as successful as his wife thinks he is." Also, "It's not the wagon that a man drives, but the woman who drives the man."

While the tragedies of war seemed to go on, other events of 1863 showed that the happier episodes of life at home go on as well. Three of the Reavis children experienced blessings during the year. In March, the oldest daughter Martha, and husband John W. Vaughan, gave birth to a son named John Lewis. In October, Lucy gave birth to a daughter named Pattie Martha. In November, one of the twin girls, Della, was asked by George Brittain Harris of Middleburg to marry him. Della was eighteen, while George was ten years her elder.

As the year drew to a close, Lewis and Mary Reavis felt blessed to still have three of their eight children safe at home with them – Ella, Mary, and John Billie. However, they knew that the Lord only gives children to be enjoyed for a season.

Chapter 14 – The Flank March

After the Battle of Sharpsburg in September 1862, T.C. was hospitalized for a period of time before being granted a sick furlough. Sam on the other hand, not being wounded, remained with the Twenty-Third Regiment and participated in its ensuing battles. The regiment was now under Alfred Iverson's Brigade, along with three other regiments: the Fifth, the Twelfth, and the Twentieth. After being encamped along Opequon Creek during most of October, in November the brigade marched southeast to Fredericksburg. Sam felt fortunate that the Twenty-Third took no active part in the Battle of Fredericksburg. This was because the regiment's assignment was to hold up in reserve near Hamilton's Crossing. The only risk to which Sam was exposed was occasional artillery fire from a distance.

After the Confederate's decisive win at Fredericksburg, the brigade went into winter quarters just outside of the city. The brigade did a great deal of shivering picket duty, as the Yankees were in full force on the opposite side of the Rappahannock River. The only notable events Sam would later tell about that harsh winter was the horseplay and snowball fights the soldiers engaged in for entertainment. The serious times were on Sunday, when the chaplains would conduct church services. Through letters from back home, Sam learned that his brother T.C. was in a Richmond hospital recovering from his wounds incurred at Sharpsburg. He also learned that his brother-in-law Alex was at home on sick furlough recovering from pneumonia.

When April finally came in 1863, the Union forces of 120,000 strong made their move. Led by General Hooker, they came across the Rappahannock River and concentrated near Chancellorsville. On May 1st and 2nd, Hooker advanced from Chancellorsville toward Lee's army. Lee gave orders for Stonewall Jackson and his 22,000 men to perform an undetected 12-mile march in order to flank Hooker's advance from the left. This flank was executed while the Union's troops were being distracted by Jeb Stuart's Calvary.

Officer Vines Turner of the Twenty-Third would later report that, "Jackson...whose very boldness bewildered the enemy, swept from Hooker's left flank across his front and fell upon the unsuspecting right flank like a bolt from the skies." Taking the lead role in this brilliant maneuver, the Twenty-Third Regiment led the vanguard.

During the flank march, Sam was apprehensive about the regiment's assignment, as the Confederates were greatly outnumbered. The Twenty-Third finally reached their assigned position in mid-afternoon. Tired, breathless, but buoyant, Sam and the men settled down in the woods. They waited their opportunity to attack, like a wildcat about to pounce. Peering through the trees, Sam could see that the Union soldiers were sitting down to dinner and had their rifles stacked. The Federalists' first clue to the impending onslaught was the observation of numerous wildlife fleeing the woods in their direction.

It was 5 o'clock in the afternoon when orders were given for the attack to commence. With the round red-orange sun setting in the west, the regiment charged from the woods at double quick. In unison, Sam and the men gave the "Rebel Yell." Little resistance was met, with the surprised enemy surrendering or breaking in the wildest rout and disorder. Chasing them like hares, the Twenty-Third boys surged forward into a big field, coming up on the rear of a line of cannons which were facing the opposite direction. The fighting lasted well into the night. In the end, prisoners, pieces of artillery, a regimental flag, and countless stands of small arms were seized by the Twenty-Third. The regiment's loss that night was small, as it had been more of a chase than a fight.

Darkness and confusion were taking their toll. The attackers were almost as disorganized as the routed defenders. When orders were finally given to withdraw, Sam and a number of other men of the Granville Rifles got separated from the regiment. In their attempt to rejoin the regiment, they twisted swiftly through a thick brush forest. Fortunately, there was a full moon to assist them in finding their way. The only things that accompanied them were fireflies that flickered in the dark, which seemed to lead them in the right direction.

As the disoriented soldiers came upon Plank Road, they met up with a small contingent of men on horseback. Cautious at first, the soldiers soon realized that the horsemen were Confederate officers. The lead horseman, who had a dark beard, asked Sam who they were. Sam responded that they were with the North Carolina Twenty-Third and were trying to rejoin their regiment. The horseman then leaned over and with his left hand, patted Sam on the shoulder. Addressing the men on the ground, the horseman said, "You men fought bravely today. With men like you, we will win this war!" With that being said, the contingent rode on.

It was only after the horses had sped off that Sam and the men realized that the horseman was General Stonewall Jackson. Little did they know that less than thirty minutes later, Jackson would be shot by men of the 18th NC Infantry, who mistook the horsemen to be part of a Yankee cavalry charge. It was midnight before Sam and the men finally rejoined the rest of their regiment.

The next day, fighting commenced again with the first skirmishes taking place at five-thirty in the morning in the woods to the left of Plank Road near Hazel Grove. The Twenty-Third was resisted fiercely by the Union troops behind strong earthworks. Sam and his fellow comrades fought for their lives and were encouraged by the presence of both Generals Robert Lee and Jeb Stuart on horseback in the rear giving orders. After two more days of fighting, the Union forces retreated altogether. However, the Twenty-Third incurred major casualties, with two big losses. Major C.C. Blacknall and Lieutenant George Bullock were both taken as prisoners. These two officers would be exchanged two weeks later, in time to take part in the Gettysburg campaign.

James T. Stone of Kittrell, who had by this time been promoted from Private to Corporal, was reported missing. Stone later rejoined the regiment, indicating that he was forced to "play possum" in a roadside ditch for nearly a day in order to avoid being captured by Federals who had completely surrounded him.

Sam was dismayed when he later heard that the wounds incurred by Stonewall Jackson on the night that he encountered him on Plank Road led to pneumonia. This condition contributed to Jackson's death eight days later on May 10. Jackson's injury was similar to the one Private T.C. Reavis experienced to his left hand at Sharpsburg, but more extensive. One of the three bullets that hit Jackson that night had entered his left hand and shattered his arm, resulting in the arm having to be amputated. While the body of Jackson would be laid to rest in Lexington, Virginia, his left arm was buried by a chaplain in the Ellwood Plantation Cemetery, not too far from the spot where he was shot.

For the rest of his life, Sam would never forget that full moon night in May of 1863 when Jackson's left hand patted him on the back, nor the fireflies that guided him to safety on Plank Road.

Chapter 15 – The Stone Wall

Considering the Battle of Chancellorsville a major victory for the Confederates, General Lee decided to once again take the fighting into Northern territory. Toward the end of June 1863, Lee concentrated his army around Gettysburg, Pennsylvania. His hopes were to win a major battle on Northern soil. While the Battle of Gettysburg would cover the first three days of July 1863, the NC Twenty-Third Regiment would only be involved in the first day's fighting. This was because the regiment was nearly annihilated the first day.

Before going to Gettysburg, Confederate General Ewell's forces went to a town just north of Gettysburg called Carlisle. Upon reaching the edge of Carlisle on June 27, General Ewell was met by a delegation of citizens under a flag of truce to arrange the surrender of the town. While camped in the town for three days, the Confederates confiscated several barrels of whiskey and had a grand time. Although Private Sam Reavis and his comrades participated in the drinking, they were embarrassed by the inebriated condition they witnessed of General Iverson, the leader of their brigade.

On July 1, General Iverson's Brigade left Carlisle and marched toward the town of Gettysburg. The brigade was comprised of four regiments: the Twenty-Third, the Fifth, the Twelfth, and the Twentieth. It was a typical hot summer day, with the sun's rays bearing down on the men. Sam noticed how ripe the cherries were on the wild cherry trees along the road. The trees reminded him of the wild cherry tree behind the horse stables back home.

The road the brigade was traveling was called Mummasburg Road. About three o'clock in the afternoon, the soldiers reached Farmer John Forney's house. At this point, the Rebels formed a perfectly straight line, with guns at right shoulder. Each of the four regiments proudly displayed their regimental flags. The Twenty-Third's flag showed that it was a veteran regiment. This was evidenced by the names of its various battles being stitched on their flag. Sam and his comrades of the Twenty-Third were in the middle of the regimental line, which stretched some 600 yards across.

General Iverson gave the orders to march and "Give them hell!" However, that was the last the brigade saw or heard of Iverson, as he did not participate in the march. Iverson's absence was due purportedly to his drunken condition. To Iverson's defense, he had suffered a wound in the groin at the Battle of Chancellorsville. Marching across the farmer's open field, the Rebels trampled a matrix wooden fence. Briars along the fence had served as good hiding places for jack rabbits that went scurrying. Sam and the men were somewhat leery of the march, as Iverson had not sent out any skirmishers to scout the position of the enemy.

As the soldiers approached the town, Sam noticed a stone wall diagonally to his left, at the top of Oak Ridge. The first thing that came to Sam's mind was the granite rocks back home on the Reavis farm near the Greystone Community. Unbeknownst to Sam and the brigade, Union troops were well hidden from sight behind the stone wall. Being no more than one hundred yards from the wall, the Yankees, lying flat on their stomachs, could actually read the names of the battles stitched on the Twenty-Third's colors. The Yankees patiently crouched, with their rifles cocked and fingers on the triggers.

As the result of the lack of leadership, the brigade veered away from the other brigades comprising Rhode's Division, exposing their left flank. This isolation gave the Federals their opportunity to launch their attack on the Rebels. The brigade was in perfect marching order when Sam heard a yell that came from behind the wall that jolted his ears. The yell was enough to make his heart stop momentarily. A Yankee officer had yelled, "Up men and Fire! Fire!"

The Federals cut loose with their first volley. Startled, Sam looked up quickly. What appeared to be coming toward him in slow motion from behind the wall was a sheet of flames and smoke. Right off the bat, nearly five-hundred exposed Rebels dropped in an even, seemingly endless row. The large number of men hit was due to the accuracy of the musket rifles at such close range. Sam heard bullets whizzing by his head as he saw the two soldiers on each side of him get hit and fall. There being nothing to take cover behind, Sam immediately dropped to the ground. The only thing he had to hug was the ground. Twenty yards ahead he saw a muddy swell in the field that looked as if it could possibly provide some type of cover. The field reminded him of a tobacco field back home that had a muddy spot where water always stood after a big rain.

Colonel Christie was already in the swell and hollered, "This way men! This way!" Sam began crawling for all he was worth. Sam soon realized that what he initially thought to be red mud was actually blood from his fallen comrades.

The row of dead men provided Sam his only cover as he crawled. Even though it took nearly two minutes to reach the sunken spot, it seemed like a lifetime. Several childhood memories went through Sam's head as he squirmed his way forward. During the crawl, he recollected the many prayers of protection his Mama had prayed over him. He stopped crawling only momentarily to cover his head when he heard a loud cannon boom. Upon looking up, he saw a jack rabbit hopping before him, as if guiding him to his destination.

For nearly an hour, unable to advance and unwilling to retreat, the surviving members of the brigade lay in the hollow. They fought the best they could, being exposed to a steady barrage of fire. Sam knew what was coming next when he heard a Yankee Officer on the other side of the wall yell, "Up boys and give them steel!" Upon seeing the Rebels trapped, Yankee regiments from Pennsylvania, New York, and Massachusetts came charging over the wall with fixed bayonets. During this bayonet attack, a Yankee clubbed the Confederate color bearer over the head and captured the prized flag of the Twenty-Third as a trophy.

At this point, a number of Confederates were captured as well, including two soldiers from Kittrell – James T. Stone and James Rial Stewart. Amid the commotion, Jonathan Fuller Coghill, also of Kittrell, grabbed Sam Reavis by the arm and said, "Follow me and do exactly as I do." Jonathan, a trained sharpshooter, began to walk slowly and nonchalantly toward the rear away from the fighting. Sam did as he was instructed and followed. Surprisingly, the two men walked off of the battlefield without being noticed.

Sam and Jonathan contributed their ability to escape partly to a diversion created by Rial Stewart. Rial had put up an amazing hand-to-hand fight that drew the attention of the astonished Yankees. Rial was finally overpowered and taken prisoner. While being taken off the field on the opposite side, Rial was shot when another line of battle came up from behind and shot into the group. Most disturbing to Sam and Jonathan was watching a Yankee take Rial's watch off his body and knowing they could do nothing to prevent the theft.

Rial lived for nearly five hours after being shot. The bullet that struck him went in the right side and came out the left side. Comforting Rial during his last hours was Kenchin Coghill, Jonathan's brother. Rial's last words were, "I now wait for that last trumpet call." Kenchin assumed the task of burying Rial's body. In a letter written home, Jonathan would later tell that Rial "was a brave and noble boy, fought like a tiger, and died in peace with a right mind." Recognized for his gallantry once the account of the battle was written, Rial was "posthumously awarded the Badge of Honor for gallantry in battle."

Sam and the survivors were put on guard detail for the rest of the battle. Colonel Daniel Christie of Henderson and Major C.C. Blacknall of Kittrell, both being wounded were taken to the Hankey house. Outside the house, the 53 surviving members of the Twenty-Third gathered, anxiously waiting to learn of their leaders' conditions. Christie had a soldier help him to the front door where he addressed the men. With all the emotion he could muster, Christie told them, "Men, I might not live to lead you in battle again, but I'll see to it that the imbecile Iverson never should either." Reports were that during the slaughter, General Iverson had been hiding behind a large chestnut log, too scared to look over it until the shooting was over.

These reports only fueled the animosity the men had toward Iverson. From the beginning they had resented a Georgian being chosen to lead the Tar Heels. It would take months before the men received satisfaction. Lee finally decided to remove Iverson as commander of the brigade and replace him with Robert Johnston of the Twenty-Third.

While Major Blacknall, shot through the mouth and neck would survive to fight another day, Christie would die of his wounds enroute to Winchester. During the retreat through South Mountain, Blacknall was captured by Kilpatrick's Union forces. Somehow or other he was able to temporarily escape. However, he was recaptured and later imprisoned at Fort McHenry near Baltimore.

Before Gettysburg, the Twenty-Third's numbers were already down to 336 due to the heavy losses at Sharpsburg and Chancellorsville. With 283 men being lost in Forney's field the first day of fighting at Gettysburg, Sam was among only 53 men still left of the regiment. Sam had always been taught by his parents that only the Lord knows the day of one's appointed time. Sam was glad to know that today was not his day. For the rest of his life, Sam would never forget his comrades killed in the swell of the field that day. The swell would later become known as Iverson's Pit, which locals to this day claim is haunted.

Flag of NC Twenty-Third Regiment
Captured by Federals at Battle of Gettysburg
July 1, 1863
(Returned to State of NC in 1905)

Photo Courtesy North Carolina Museum of History

Chapter 16 - Retreat South

After Gettysburg, the Confederates headed south back toward Virginia. With over 500 wagons of wounded and supplies, the troops passed through Hagerstown, Maryland. Three days later on July 6, the Twenty Third arrived at Hagerstown, a town of about 4,000 citizens. There the regiment encountered fighting already taking place involving Virginia regiments and Union cavalrymen. Although worn and tattered, the Tar Heels were enough reinforcements to drive the Yankees out of town.

During the encounter, just after 3 o'clock in the afternoon, Sam was positioned on Potomac Street near the town square. Seeing the blue-coated cavalrymen in the square, he fired toward them. He was in the process of reloading when he saw a rifle aimed directly at him. Once again Sam's heart stopped, fearing a bullet was about to strike him. Wanting to take cover, he couldn't, as his feet seemed to freeze under him. Then all of a sudden, Sam heard a shot from a second story window of a dwelling close by. The cavalryman with the rifle aimed at Sam fell to his death in front of him.

Looking up, Sam saw a young girl standing in the window. He was first struck at the sight of her long blonde hair. Then he saw the rifle in her hands she had used to shoot the Yankee, very likely saving Sam's life. The angelic girl blew Sam a kiss and stepped back away from the window out of sight.

Sam then saw the steeple of Saint John's Lutheran Church, which reminded him to pause and say a brief prayer of thanksgiving. Sam later learned that the dwelling from which the girl shot the Yankee belonged to a Doctor Dorsey. Years later, Sam would write a letter to the Doctor's daughter thanking her for saving his life on that hot July day in 1863.

The following day, the NC Fifty-Fourth Regiment, a part of General Imboden's Division, arrived from Williamsport and converged with Lee's main Army. For the first time since the war had started, Sam Reavis of the Twenty-Third and his brother-in-law Alex Wortham of the Fifty-Fourth Regiment were in the same vicinity.

On July 9, Sam obtained a one-day furlough in order to visit the camp of the Fifty-Fourth Regiment to visit Alex. The two camps were no more than five miles apart at this point. Upon arriving at the camp, Sam had to obtain the permission of the Captain of Company K, Samuel Jones Parham of Henderson. This was no problem, as Captain Parham was his first cousin, being the son of Delia Hawkins Reavis. Captain Parham was overjoyed to see Sam.

Alex was both happy and surprised to see Sam, as Alex had no idea whether or not Sam had survived Gettysburg. The two family members spent three hours together, eating grub and sharing with each other their recent battle adventures. Sam chuckled as he asked Alex, "Do you think our grandchildren will ever know about these battles we have fought in?" Alex replied, "Maybe, if one of us lives long enough to tell." The one positive thing they could agree on was that they were thankful they were not back in Granville County working in the hot tobacco fields.

Alex did have one important request of Sam, "Should anything happen to me, will you please ensure the welfare of Lucy and our child she is carrying?" Alex had already told Sam that his wife Lucy was expecting in October. Obviously, Sam told him that he would. Neither one of them knew that this time together would be the last that they would share with each other, and that Sam would one day have to carry through on his promise.

For the next three hot summer months of 1863, the fighting for both regiments drifted south. There were a number of brief engagements, including ones close to Orange Courthouse, Madison Courthouse, Culpepper Courthouse, Warren Springs, and Brandy Station. For both men, much of their time was spent on fatigue duty, either being on picket or tearing up railroad track. Alex had recuperated from pneumonia by this time. However, he was still suffering from severe rheumatism, which the hard railroad labor was not helping at all. Tired of fighting, both men were looking forward to going into winter quarters with their respective regiment.

While at Orange Courthouse, three divisions formed a review for General Lee's inspection. Not only was General Lee inspecting the men, but a large group of town girls showed up to inspect the several thousands of soldiers in the three lines as well. Sam noted that the girls paid close attention to the men's coat collars. The men with the most stripes and stars seemed to be the ones who got the most admiration.

Much of the picketing during this time took place along the Rapidan River. The Yankees were camped on the north side while the Confederates were camped on the south side. During this season of unofficial cease fire, the soldiers on one side would occasionally talk with the soldiers on the other side, and even exchange newspapers. Each set of soldiers would see its enemy some thirty yards on the other side of the river washing their hands and faces. Sam kept wondering just how long this friendly stand-off would last, as he knew bloodshed would eventually erupt.

September of 1863 finally arrived. The fall foliage in the Shenandoah Valley was some of the prettiest Sam Reavis had ever seen, much more spectacular than that in the piedmont of North Carolina. He was awe struck with the majestic creation of the Lord and recognized that he was part of that creation. The shimmering sunshine, the colorful flowers, the spectacular wildlife, the smell of the scuppernong grapes, and the sound of the running brooks all evoked a closer awareness of God and his relationship with Him.

While the mountain area was not heaven, Sam realized he was venturing on a journey through life that would eventually bring him to the entrance of heaven. He did not know when he would arrive at that destination in the celestial sky. However, he knew that the Lord was preparing him for it each step of the way while here on earth.

This spiritual awareness was contagious, as the first two weeks of September 1863 saw a revival occur throughout the entire brigade. Camp meetings were held every night, being led mostly by chaplains. One night alone Sam saw thirty men profess religion. Another night there was an additional seventy men to make the profession. The following Sunday all one-hundred converts were baptized in the river.

It was during these two weeks of revival that Sam realized God moves in mysterious ways. Many of the men who would die over the following months and years would not have obtained everlasting life if the war had not placed them in a position where they were confronted with the prospect of dying any day. The preaching opened their hearts to the truth regarding the possibility of being condemned to everlasting damnation. The single question that each soldier was faced with answering was: "Where will you spend eternity?"

The war would have two positive results. Not only would the Negroes receive their freedom from slavery, but many lost souls would find freedom in Christ. Unfortunately, the liberty associated with states' rights would forever be suppressed.

Chapter 17 – Taken Prisoner

Lee's plans were for the Northern Army of Virginia to go into winter quarters in November 1863. However, General George Meade was being pressured by President Lincoln to continue the pursuit of the Confederates as they went south. On November 7, Meade aggressively moved against Lee, with attacks at both Rappahannock Station and Kelly's Ford. Confederate artillery was positioned on the hills south of the Rappahannock River and was engaged in artillery fire with Union artillery positioned on the north side. Most of the Confederate troops were forced to retreat to the south side of the river.

As dusk arrived, the fighting seemingly stopped. Two thousand Confederates were still positioned on the north side of the river at Rappahannock Station, with the assignment of protecting the bulkhead of a pontoon bridge. A surprise attack that night resulted in the massive capture of more than 1,600 Rebels. The other 400 Confederates escaped the disaster, many by swimming the frigid waters of the

Rappahannock River. The Confederate troops on the south side of the river could only watch the fate of their comrades on the north side as they were being captured. They also witnessed the drowning of a number of comrades who were swallowed up by the river.

The troops on guard at Rappahannock Station included the NC Fifty-Fourth Regiment. Alex Wortham was on picket duty that night. It was a cool brisk night, and Alex was doing his best to keep warm. He had just received a letter from his wife Lucy that day telling him he was the father of a little baby girl. Her name was Pattie Martha, born three weeks earlier on October 16. This news from home had pre-occupied his mind all day.

When the surprise attack occurred, there was little time to respond. Alex thought about jumping into the river along with those who elected to do so that night. However, not being a good swimmer, this did not appear to be an option. Captured along with Alex was Captain Samuel Parham, his wife's cousin.

Also captured that same night, but further downstream at Kelly's Ford, was Private John Jeremiah Pegram of the NC Thirtieth Regiment. Before the war, a number of times John Jeremiah had called on Ella Reavis, the sister of Alex's wife. Ella was one of the twin girls that grew up in the Reavis House. Since John Jeremiah's enlistment in August of 1861, he and Ella had been writing letters to each other.

For the next four days, the 1,600 prisoners, including twenty officers, were marched to Point Lookout in Maryland. This Northern prison was situated on a peninsula where the Chesapeake Bay and Potomac River met. As Alex marched, he could only imagine what prison life would be like. Alex was somewhat encouraged after talking to John Jeremiah, who had previously been captured at Frederick in September 1862. John Jeremiah was fortunate to have been exchanged after only five weeks of incarceration at Fort Delaware. While Alex was hopeful his incarceration would be short-lived, such short-term exchanges were no longer commonplace in 1863. This was because the Federals had discovered that, while Union prisoners once released went home, Confederate prisoners once released went back to the battlefield. The occasional humming of the song Dixie by the prisoners kept the men somewhat upbeat as they marched.

On November 11, 1863, the prisoners arrived at their destination, reportedly the largest Union-run prison camp in the North. Alex would soon find out that it was also one of the worst prisons. The capacity of the prison was supposedly 10,000 men, but the number of inmates sometimes exceeded 20,000. As the men approached the prison, which appeared to cover about forty acres, they could see that the wooden fence surrounding the area was about fifteen feet high, with a gallery along the top for the guards.

Alex was shocked to discover that the prisoners' sleeping quarters would be tents instead of barracks. Up to sixteen men would occupy a single tent. The tents were set up in parallel streets running east to west. The inmates named the main path running through the center of the prison, "Pennsylvania Avenue." Being close to the bay, the composition of the ground was mostly sand, and there was no vegetation whatsoever.

As each prisoner was processed, he was identified as either an "enlisted prisoner" or an "officer prisoner." Being privates, Alex and John Jeremiah were assigned to the section of tents designated for enlisted prisoners. Captain Samuel Parham was assigned to the section of tents designated for officer prisoners. The two sections were separated by a fence between them. In addition to Confederate soldiers, a number of Maryland citizens who were Southern sympathizers were imprisoned there.

The guards were from various Union regiments that rotated in and out. When Alex arrived, the guards consisted of two regiments from New Hampshire. Later on, all guard details would consist almost entirely of Colored regiments. There were a few cases where a Colored guard would find himself guarding his former master. Such an occurrence could be either good or bad for the inmate, depending on how the master had treated the slave prior to the war.

Most guards were extremely strict, and the inmates discovered early on that the guards were easily provoked. Animosity was readily shown, as the guards would frequently remind the inmates that they were incarcerated for killing Northerners. Several times, Alex witnessed prisoners being shot by the guards. Shootings would occur when inmates either purposely or accidentally ventured across the "dead line." This was an invisible line marking the edge of a ten-foot border around the inside of the prison fence. Alex also learned pretty quickly to keep quiet at night, as it was common for prisoners to be randomly shot by the guards as they slept, or if they called out from pain.

Living conditions were "worse than terrible," more so than any of the prisoners had ever experienced as a citizen or soldier. Fresh water for drinking was scarce and polluted. Water from the prison wells contained iron and alkaline salts. Meals were served twice per day, which was never enough to satisfy the inmates' hunger. The inmates often made a sport out of catching rats in the prison, since they were a major source of protein. There was a daily roll call every day after breakfast to see who had survived the night. Attempting to escape was not even contemplated, as the few who tried were shot.

Due primarily to the unsanitary conditions, disease was rampant. Chronic diarrhea, dysentery and typhoid fever had become epidemic at the prison. Smallpox, malaria, scurvy, and the itch were common diseases. In addition to sick tents, there was a series of buildings situated in a spoke fashion serving as a hospital. On average, there were four to five deaths every day, either from wounds incurred in battle or disease contracted while incarcerated.

Exposure to the harsh weather would sometimes be the cause of death. This was because there was hardly enough firewood during the winter months. Being very close to sea level, the camp was subject to flooding, causing what few blankets there were to be soaked. There was no such thing as cots, only the hard ground to sleep on.

Back home, Alex's wife Lucy and the Reavis Family learned of the capture of Alex and John Jeremiah. They had heard stories of the ill-treatment that was prevalent in Federal prisons and were even more appalled when they learned of a law the United States Congress enacted making the poor treatment of prisoners the official policy of the Federal government. The official U.S. policy on Confederate POWs was stated in the preamble to HR 97: "Rebel prisoners in our hands are to be subjected to a treatment finding its parallels only in the conduct of savage tribes and resulting in the death of multitudes by the slow but designed process of starvation and by mortal diseases occasioned by insufficient and unhealthy food and wanton exposure of their persons to the inclemency of the weather."

Captain Parham would stay at Point Lookout for only a short period of time before being transferred. Over the course of the next year, Parham would be confined in six other prisons. Being an officer, he would be used as a political pawn. While confined in a stockade in Morris Island, SC, he was among the "Immortal Six Hundred." This was the name given to a group of Confederate Officers so arranged in line at the fort such that they were exposed to artillery fire from their own forces. This incident was widely publicized and aroused great indignation in the South. Captain Parham would be paroled and exchanged at Charleston Harbor, SC on December 15, 1864. He would return to Henderson, become the town mayor, and marry Maria Southerland. Maria Parham Hospital would later be named for her.

Private John Jeremiah Pegram would stay at Point Lookout for just over five months before being part of a prisoner exchange in April 1864. John Jeremiah went home to Warren County and had a four-month stay. During this time he called on his sweetheart Ella Reavis, with whom he had fallen in love through their correspondence. But at the end of August, he felt his duty was to return to his regiment to continue fighting for the cause. Five months later he would be wounded in the left arm at Petersburg. He would be hospitalized in Richmond until furloughed in February of 1865.

Alex on the other hand, would remain imprisoned at Point Lookout for ten months until September 1864. Having developed chronic diarrhea and in poor health, Alex was a candidate for being exchanged to make room for more recently captured Confederates arriving from the Third Battle of Winchester. In September, Alex indeed was paroled and exchanged. Hearing that some of the new prisoners enroute were from the Twenty-Third Regiment, Alex was hopeful that his brother-in-law Sam Reavis would not be one of them. Imprisonment in that hell hole was something Alex would not even wish on his worst enemy. Alex would never know if Sam was among the arriving inmates, as the new prisoners would not arrive until five days after Alex was paroled from the prison on September 18.

Alex's exchange took place September 22 at Aiken's Landing on the James River, just north of Varina, Virginia. On the day of the exchange, the Confederate inmates came down the gang plank from the transport ship at the dock. They were a gruesome sight, with bodies resembling skeletons, and eyes that appeared lusterless. Some of the men departed from the ship on crutches while others had to be carried off by their comrades.

Like many of those coming down the gang plank, Alex's face displayed the seal of death, characterized by sunken cheeks from malnutrition. Somehow, Alex knew his appointed time was near. Having been baptized as a child at Geneva Presbyterian Church in Granville County, he was able to accept his predestined fate. While he had every reason to hate the Yankees for his mistreatment while imprisoned, he knew the Christian thing to do was to forgive them. He did not want to carry a grudge to the grave and have to give account for it when he met his Lord.

What he feared most was the agony of dying alone amid enemies in a foreign land. Now, just being on Southern soil amid people of compassion was a comfort to him.

Two days after being set free, Alex was admitted to a Richmond hospital for his chronic diarrhea condition. The hospital was familiar to him, as he had been hospitalized there with pleurisy and pneumonia the prior winter. Alex would not recover. He died within a week of arrival at the hospital.

The night before Alex's death, an angel appeared to him in a dream. The angel spoke softly, "Alex, your purpose here on earth is near completion. However, future generations will one day learn of your love for your parents, for your wife, and for your daughter. The news of this love, of your endurance, of your forgiving spirit, and of your profession of faith as a child at Geneva Presbyterian Church will be a witness to future generations."

The only part of the angel's message that Alex could comprehend was that the day had arrived for him to meet his Lord. He did not understand how his life could possibly be a witness to future generations. This was because he figured he would be buried without even a tombstone, and within a few years the memory of his life would be lost to the wind.

Alex's body indeed never was returned to Granville County, but was interred somewhere in the Richmond Confederate Cemetery. His main death bed regret was that he never had the opportunity to see his daughter. Pattie, conceived during his last furlough, was almost one year old now. With no family at his side, Alex died in peace, committing his soul to the Lord. His last thoughts were knowing that he was passing on to the other side to await the future arrival of his wife Lucy, who was being left a widow at the age of 26.

Chapter 18 – Spring Fighting Resumes

Lee's Army had gone into winter quarters in the late fall of 1863, south of the Rapidan River. Although the Fifty-Fourth Regiment was involved in the Battle of Rappahannock Station on November 8, where Alex Wortham was taken prisoner, the Twenty-Third was not involved in the battle. Consequently, Sam Reavis avoided the possibility of being captured. Sam was thankful he had survived Gettysburg earlier that summer. He was also glad to learn that his brother T.C. was detailed as a provost guard in Raleigh, due to his wounds incurred at Sharpsburg. However, Sam was distressed knowing that his brother-in-law Alex was imprisoned at Point Lookout.

It was during this winter break that Sam was granted an eighteen-day furlough. On February 25, 1864, Sam left camp and made his way to Richmond There he was able to catch a train to Henderson. Knowing it would take a week to get home and nearly a week to return to camp, he would have a week at the most to spend in North Carolina. He decided to take advantage of the opportunity and embarked upon the journey. He was anxious to get home as he had not seen his family in nearly three years. The trip went without any hitch. For five days in March, Sam enjoyed being in Granville County with his family. With Sam being an eligible bachelor, the girls in the community gave him plenty of attention. He returned to camp from his furlough without a day to spare.

In the spring of 1864, the Twenty-Third was detached to guard bridges over the North and South Anna rivers, near Hanover Court House. In barracks at Taylorsville, with no enemy near, camp conditions were the best Sam had experienced since the war started. Unlike imprisoned Alex at this time, Sam was enjoying adequate clothing and food, even barracks to sleep in. However, Sam knew the break was only temporary. There were reports that the Federals were building up forces on the north side of the Rapidan River. Anticipation was that a Union attack was eminent.

In May, General Grant, now Commander-in-Chief of the Federal forces, indeed did initiate an offensive against Lee's Army. This confrontation in the thick woods was known as the Battle of the Wilderness. On May 4, the Twenty-Third left Taylorsville and by the quickest march on record, covered sixty-six miles in twenty-three hours. They arrived at the Plank Road near the Wilderness Tavern on May 5.

Sam had not spent so much energy since Gettysburg ten months earlier. Fighting in the dense woods was already underway. The Twenty-Third, now under Gordon's Brigade, came in as reinforcements. Dead tired from the march, the Confederates were still able to drive the Federals back. When Sam finally did get a chance to sleep, he slept like a log.

The next engagement for the Twenty-Third, now under General Johnson's Brigade, was at Spotsylvania Courthouse on May 9. After initially driving back a Division of Burnside, Johnston's Brigade was forced to withdraw. This retreat was a result of being nearly enveloped by the enemy in overwhelming force. No time passed at all that same day before the brigade fought and ran off a heavy cavalry force endeavoring to hold the high ground around the old court house at Spotsylvania. The Union cavalry was a splendid body and fought desperately. However, no incident of war was more relished by Sam and the Rebel boys than their trouncing and chasing the blue-coated horsemen that spring day.

The fighting the next day on May 10 was perhaps the most inspiring that Sam would experience in the war. As sunset approached, Union troops broke over the Confederate line of artillery works and were advancing rapidly toward General Lee's headquarters in the field. Johnston's brigade did a double-quick and concealed itself behind a pine thicket. Sam and the Confederates crouched in wait, being reminded of how the Yankees had waited to ambush them at Gettysburg.

At the commander's signal, emerging suddenly from the pines, Sam and his comrades initiated a counter-attack that drove the enemy back across the breastworks. The artillery pieces that had just been lost hours before were regained. The cannons were used effectively against the retreating Federals.

Sam then witnessed a sight he would long remember. Just as the Rebels were making the charge toward the fleeing Yankees, Sam saw General Lee on horseback. Lee was no more than 100 yards of the enemy, hat in hand, cheering on the men. Not until 9 o'clock that night did the fighting cease.

In the process, a Federal flag was captured by the Confederates as a trophy.

May 11 turned out to be a day of relief for the Twenty-Third, as the regiment was held in reserve. However, fighting continued over the next four days, with heavy losses being incurred at a place which became known as the "Bloody Angle." Some of the Twenty-Third were killed, wounded, or captured. Sam was one of those who were wounded, although his injury was only a flesh wound.

The wounded were transported to Wayside Hospital in Richmond, arriving there on May 13. The hospital, which was a converted tobacco warehouse, was located on Grace Street near the railroad station. Not really wanting to go to the hospital, Sam was ordered to go anyway. Sam was grateful to be treated and discharged the next day. This allowed him to return to duty in time to participate in the March to Washington City.

It had been a long spring for Sam, having been engaged in battle for what seemed to be nearly every day. He now had an arsenal of battle stories to hopefully tell his grandchildren someday. And yet, there was more to be experienced.

Chapter 19 – March to Washington City

The month of June 1864 found Private Sam Reavis and the Twenty-Third joining General Early's Regiment in the mission of marching to Washington City. Such an endeavor was a bold move, as it had been almost a year since the Confederates were defeated in the North at Gettysburg. The regiment marched from camp at Cold Harbor to Charlottesville, where they boarded railroad cars and headed to Lynchburg. The regiment arrived in Lynchburg just in time to ward off an attack on the town from Union General Hunter's forces. Fighting commenced just twenty minutes after deboarding the train. This defensive action helped in saving the Confederate vital rail center. Shooting and being shot at had now become a routine for Sam.

After skirmishing at Liberty and driving General Hunter's forces across Salem and toward the mountains, the regiment called for a vote to make a detour to see the Natural Bridge. By a small majority vote of the curious, the regiment made the detour and spent several hours of rest beneath the natural wonder. Sam was one of those who voted for the detour. He cast his positive vote because of his interest in unique rock formations. Being adventurous, he had also remembered learning in school that George Washington had placed his mark on the rock wall beneath the bridge when he had surveyed the area as a young man.

The regiment pushed on to Staunton and then passed by Harper's Ferry, with only a few skirmishes being engaged. On July 9, in the steaming heat, the regiment engaged in fighting at Monocacy Junction near Fredericksburg, Maryland. Union General Wallace's forces made a determined stand at the Monocacy River in an attempt to prevent the regiment from crossing and marching to Washington.

By this time, Colonel Blacknall had rejoined the regiment after being released from Johnson's Island Prison in Lake Erie. Sam was glad to have the Colonel as his leader once again. Blacknall led an attack on a block house near the railroad, but the initial attack failed and the regiment had to fall back. Eventually, the Confederates prevailed, with the Union forces retreating. This Confederate victory opened the way for the Rebels to continue their march to Washington City.

About three o'clock in the afternoon of Monday, July 11, the Confederates arrived in sight of the Federal Capital. The day was one of overpowering heat. The troops were too exhausted with hard marching to have been effective in an immediate attack. Sam was use to the hot tobacco fields of Granville County, but the heat that day was more than he could bear. It was even hotter than that awful day at the Battle of Gettysburg a year earlier.

The brigade had camped in a grove of trees adjacent to the three Blair mansions located in the area of Silver Spring,

Maryland. That night, some of the Confederate troops looted the home of Montgomery Blair, finding barrels of whiskey in the basement of the mansion. Sam had learned his lesson from a similar incident prior to Gettysburg and did not participate in the drinking. This episode resulted in the troops not being able to get an early morning start the next day, as well as allowing for further fortification by Union troops.

It was around noon on July 12, as the men were eating in the camp at Silver Spring, when an 11-inch shell from Fort Stevens landed in the midst of the Twenty-Third Regiment. No one was hurt, but the plate of food Sam was holding was knocked out of his hands. Later that day, the mansion known as Falkland mysteriously burned to the ground. While some blamed the Confederates for the burning, Sam always contended that the mansion was ignited by shells from the forts that made his regiment their target that day.

Sam was a member of the skirmishers who made a reconnaissance on Tuesday, but the Union artillery works were too strongly manned for the 10,000 Confederates to carry. Participating in the reconnaissance with Sam was Melville Holmes. Sam and Holmes had enlisted in the Granville Rifles on the same day back in Kittrell three years earlier. Holmes was a brave lad, attempting to sneak up on the enemy's breastworks. Sam followed close by. Upon being spotted by the enemy, a firefight broke out. Holmes was shot and killed right in front of Sam. Some claim that Melville came the closest to reaching the artillery of Fort Stevens than any other Confederate soldier of the war. Rumors were that President Lincoln was nearby watching the battle as it unfolded.

The skirmishing continued late into the day. General Early finally decided that Washington City could not be taken without heavy losses. Therefore, under the cover of darkness the Confederates then retreated. They passed swiftly through Rockville and Poolesville and crossed over the Potomac at White Ford. The brigade took a brief rest at Leesburg before marching back toward Shenandoah Valley.

For three solid months during the Spring-Summer of 1864, Sam had been engaged in battles in Virginia, Maryland, and Washington. It was now July 1864, and Sam was getting weary. He was wondering just how long this war would last. His youthful thirst for adventure had by now been quenched. He had turned 21 years of age on July 18, officially making him a man. However, the battles had contributed more to his manhood than his becoming of age.

Chapter 20 – Captured While on Picket

Retreating from Washington City in mid-July 1864, Johnston's Brigade headed toward Shenandoah Valley. The brigade passed through Snicker's Gap and arrived at Berryville, where temporary camp was set up. On the night of July 19, the Twenty-Third moved back to Winchester to help protect the town from Federals. Engagements with Union General Crook's forces occurred at Stephenson Depot on July 20 and at Kernstown on July 24. These engagements resulted in the Confederates driving the Yankees out of the Valley back across the Potomac. While most of the heavy fighting was done by the Confederate Cavalry, Private Sam Reavis and his fellow infantrymen engaged in ground support maneuvers.

The month of August consisted of periodic skirmishes with Union General Sheridan's forces. It was also a time for harvesting grain for food, herding beef cattle, and gathering supplies, tasks at which Sam was very adept. The month of September brought on fighting which would later be known as the Third Battle of Winchester.

On Sunday night September 18, Ramseur's Division was camped on the Berryville Pike east of Winchester. Johnston's Brigade was in advance with the Twenty-Third Regiment thrown out on picket near the edge of the woods that skirted the Opequon Creek. Being on picket was a duty that Sam did not mind. While there was risk, he perceived it as better than facing the Yankee Cavalry on the battlefield. Sam's position was a little north of the pike, about a mile from the tributary stream. As the enemy was known to be in force in the area, Colonel C.C. Blacknall cautioned the regiment to be on high alert.

The forest had all kinds of sounds that night, including the hoot of an owl. It crossed Sam's mind that the owl's hooting could perhaps be an omen of a pending family member's death. Sam's brother-in-law Alex, imprisoned at Point Outlook and in critical condition at the time, was on the verge of death. It was a belief among some Southerners that the death of a family member was eminent when the hoot of an owl at midnight was seemingly only heard by one individual.

Sam's thoughts also drifted toward his family back home in Granville County. Being single, he wondered if he would survive the war and ever be in the position to marry and have a family. He thought about one of the girls back home he once had an eye on at church. Sallie Margaret Baskett lived in the Spring Valley Community across Indian Creek from the Reavis House. Being somewhat shy, Sam had never actually courted Sallie, but was now determined to do so should he survive the war. From letters back home, Sam learned that his younger teenaged brother John Billie was fond of Sallie's teenaged sister, Rebecca. Sam chuckled to himself as he thought of the possibility of two brothers marrying two sisters.

Falling asleep while on picket was not an option, as punishment for such an offense could be that of facing a firing squad. It seemed as though the night would never come to an end, but yet it did. The sun was just coming up from behind the mountain range and the fog was dense. Suddenly and without a warning, out of the ravine swarmed Sheridan's troopers. Their appearance was so quick that neither Sam nor any of his comrades had time to fire before the horsemen were in their midst. An overwhelming force of cavalry, closely followed by infantry, charged the surprised pickets. Sam got one shot off before finding himself surrounded by two cavalrymen.

Sam's eyes locked onto the eyes of one of the Yankees. For a brief moment, each of the two men realized that they were looking not at an enemy, but at a fellow human being. Sam could easily have been shot, or stricken dead with a sword. There but by the grace of God the cavalryman staring him in the eyes hollered, "Surrender or die!" Not wanting to meet his Maker just yet, Sam dropped his musket and raised both arms in surrender. He repeated a phrase he had often heard others say in similar situations: "Is there no help for the widow's son?" Sam was immediately taken prisoner. The same fate befell other comrades that surrounded Sam. Altogether, the total number of Confederates taken prisoner that day was a massive 2,500.

Just before Sam's capture, he witnessed Colonel C.C. Blacknall riding up on horseback giving his men orders. It appeared to Sam that Blacknall was perhaps shot before he sped away. Sam would later learn that Blacknall had indeed been shot in the ankle and was taken to the rear for treatment. Blacknall was in too bad a shape to travel when the Confederates were forced to retreat from Winchester.

Colonel Blacknall ended up at the Waverly Farm where he was nursed by a Mrs. Washington. Unfortunately, his right foot had to be amputated. However, it was complications from intestinal and digestive problems that led to his death on November 6. Like a cat with nine lives, Blacknall had used all his lives up. Blacknall's remains would be laid to rest in Stonewall Cemetery in Winchester near his friend and comrade, Colonel Daniel Christie.

Years later, visitors to the Waverly House where Blacknall died would tell of a ghostly Confederate soldier that was occasionally seen in the upstairs window overlooking the battlefield. His memory would live on back in Kittrell as the result of the local United Daughters of the Confederacy naming their chapter after him.

Just like his brother-in-law Alex Wortham ten months earlier, Private Sam Reavis would now be marched to Point Lookout Prison in Maryland. As he marched, Sam had mixed emotions. He had heard the horrific stories of the mistreatment of prisoners at Point Lookout, something he had hoped he would never experience. On the other hand, he was somewhat hopeful over the possibility of seeing Alex.

It was September 23, 1864 when Sam and the some 2,500 prisoners arrived and were processed at Point Lookout. Captured and imprisoned along with Sam was Private John A. Harris of Warren County. Harris had experienced some troublesome times during his military career. He had deserted prior to the Battle of Sharpsburg. However, he was later arrested and reinstated. He was both wounded and captured at the Battle of Gettysburg, and later exchanged before being captured again at Winchester. Harris was drawn to Sam because Sam did not judge him for his history of desertion as some soldiers did. On the contrary, Sam admired him for his come-back spirit and was willing to give him a second chance.

For several days, Sam Reavis and John Harris attempted to locate Alex by inquiring of various inmates. Not until the third day did Sam finally run into an inmate at mess time that knew Alex. The inmate informed Sam that Alex had been paroled on September 18, just five days before Sam's arrival at the prison. While this was good news to Sam, he was disturbed to learn that Alex's chronic diarrhea condition was grave when he was released, the likely reason for his early release. It would be a month before Sam learned that Alex had passed away in a Richmond hospital on September 28. Alex's death was only ten days after he was released from Point Lookout.

While Sam had been forewarned about the conditions of the prison, the reality of what he was about to endure was beyond his imagination. Sam would be exposed to the same unhealthy conditions and cruel treatment that Alex had been exposed to over the prior ten months. Sam however was fortunate to have John Harris as one of his tent mates. The friendship of Sam and John, and their mutual support, helped each other endure the hardships for the remainder of their confinement.

In March 1865, six months after Sam Reavis and John Harris were confined at Point Lookout, 35-year old Corporal James T. Stone of Kittrell arrived at the prison, after being captured at the Battle of Fort Stedman. Sam looked up to James Stone as a leader. It was Stone, a private at the time, who had helped Sam carry T.C. Reavis off the battlefield at the Battle of Sharpsburg. Stone was also marching with Sam when the regiment was ambushed at Gettysburg.

While Sam had survived Gettysburg, Stone was both wounded and captured there. This resulted in Stone's imprisonment for three months at Davids Island in New York. While imprisoned, Stone was treated in the prison hospital for his hip wound before he was exchanged. The imprisonment at Point Lookout was the second time Stone had experienced being an inmate in a Federal prison.

Sam would be exchanged on March 18, 1865 at Aiken's Landing on the James River. However, both Private John Harris and Corporal James Stone would not be released until they were paroled at the war's end, after taking the Oath of Allegiance on June 20, 1865.

The Twenty-Third Regiment would continue its fighting for the reminder of the war, but without Private Sam Reavis, Private John Harris, and Corporal James Stone. The three of them would miss experiencing the surrender at Appomattox in April 1865, in which 82 members of the Twenty-Third Regiment, only 35 of which were armed, took part.

Chapter 21 – Provost Guard Detail

It was July 8, 1863 when Private T.C. Reavis of the Twenty-Third Regiment reported to Camp Holmes in Raleigh, being detailed as a provost guard. This detail was the result of a Special Order he had received from the Under Secretary of War, due to wounds he incurred at the Battle of Sharpsburg. T.C. had spent the last three months at home in Granville County by virtue of having been granted a sick furlough in April. Somehow or other, T.C. had managed to overstay his furlough by almost two months before he was ordered to report to duty in Raleigh. When T.C. arrived in Raleigh, he was unaware of the horrible battle that had just ensued at Gettysburg the prior week.

Camp Holmes was primarily a conscription camp set up to indoctrinate new soldiers who were drafted into the Confederate Army as a result of the passage of the Conscription Act of 1862. The camp was located along the Raleigh and Gaston Railroad, two and one-half miles northeast of the State Capitol. The site was near the fork of two main roads, one that led to the Millbrook Community and one that led to Forestville. The camp was situated on the north bank of Buffaloe Creek, not far from two well-known houses in Raleigh – the Mordecai House to the south and the Crabtree Plantation House to the north. Not too far south of the camp was a neighborhood that was known as "Smoky Hollow," a residential area for mill workers.

The camp was manned by the "Provost Guards," a special class of troops comprised primarily of soldiers wounded in the line of duty and no longer able to serve on the front lines. They were assigned to maintain order, similar to military police, and to guard prisoners, deserters, and arrested bounty jumpers. A bounty jumper was a soldier who would desert one regiment, and fraudulently rejoin another regiment in order to collect a second enlistment signing bonus. Camp Holmes in Raleigh, a sister camp of Camp Vance in Morganton and of Camp Stokes in Greensboro, was under the jurisdiction of Major Peter Mallett's Battalion. The company of provost guards stationed at the camp numbered generally around sixty-five men.

When Private T.C. Reavis arrived at Camp Holmes, he reported to Captain Samuel B. Waters. T.C. was issued a special uniform and a badge, which were designed to distinguish provost guards from regular soldiers. In addition to his $11 per month military pay, he was also given a clothing allowance. Captain Waters was blunt when he told T.C. that his assignment at the camp would be difficult. Waters warned him first that provost guards were sorely resented by most rank and file Confederate soldiers, as well as by most citizens. First of all, some soldiers felt provost guards were shunning their battle duties by hiding behind their injuries. Second, some soldiers disliked the military police role and special powers afforded the provost guards.

One good thing about T.C. being stationed in Raleigh was the close proximity to his home in Granville County, 45 miles away. Not only was he able to occasionally take several days furlough allowing him to visit his family, but his family members could also visit him in Raleigh. Additionally, he was able to keep up with the status of his brother Sam and his brother-in-law Alex in their military travels. During T.C.'s tenure in Raleigh, both Sam and Alex would, at different times be captured and be imprisoned at Point Lookout in Maryland.

T.C.'s first assignment was to serve as a member of a squad which escorted fifteen bounty jumpers and deserters from Raleigh to Andersonville Prison located in Georgia. Upon the men's entry through the front gates of the 16-acre prison, T.C. was just as horrified as the prisoners that he escorted there. What the men saw before them were inmates who appeared to be walking skeletons. The inmates were as filthy as any hogs T.C. had ever seen in a pig pen. In the center of the prison camp was a swamp area. The scent of human excrement was suffocating. One of the arriving inmates exclaimed, "Can this be hell? God help us!"

Without delay, the escort squad left the camp as soon as they had made their delivery and had received a written receipt. T.C. thought to himself how thankful he was that he did not have to endure such a hell hole. He had heard that conditions at Federal prisons were just as bad. Little did he know that his brother Sam and brother-in-law Alex would later have to undergo such a prison sentence in a Maryland prison. In the case of Andersonville, after the war

Confederate Commander Henry Wierz would be tried and convicted of war crimes relating to the conditions at the Georgia prison. The sentencing resulted in him being hanged.

Upon T.C.'s return to Raleigh from Georgia, he participated in street patrols, primarily to check the furlough passes of off-duty soldiers. Being a major transportation center, Raleigh was a hub of many soldiers passing through the city. Soldiers without passes were suspected of being deserters, the numbers of which were growing at this phase of the war. Another duty of the street patrols was to ensure that the soldiers did not frequent off-limit saloons and houses of ill-repute. While there were several brothels in Smoky Hollow, most off-duty soldiers seeking loving attention ventured to Kinston, where they frequented the Sugar Hill District. For three dollars, a soldier could be thoroughly entertained.

One of T.C.'s most disliked duties was the capture of deserters. Talking with many of the deserters, T.C. learned that the main reason for their desertion was the choosing of loyalty to home and family over loyalty to the Confederate cause. Confederate soldiers fought for home, motherhood, and family. But as Confederate armies became less able to protect these institutions, Confederate soldiers began to reassess to what they gave their loyalty. Nevertheless, President Davis was insistent that deserters were to be punished, and T.C. was obliged to perform his duty.

One big challenge for T.C. was when the Provost Guards had to deal with the rioting in the Raleigh streets that took place September 9 through 11 of 1863. The Editor of the *Standard Newspaper*, William W. Holden had written several anti-Confederate editorials, which infuriated not only many citizens, but soldiers as well. Holden had become one of the main proponents of the peace movement, believing that there was no use in continuing to fight the war.

The riots started on the night of September 9 when Georgia soldiers passing through the city wrecked the newspaper's offices, showing their disdain of the peace editorials. This destruction incited Raleigh citizens who were supporters of Holden. The next night, in retaliation a mob of citizens destroyed the offices of the *State Journal*, whose editor was more loyal to the Confederate cause.

Private T.C. Reavis was dispatched to the quarters of General Benning at the train depot to investigate and request assistance of the Georgia soldiers in calming the situation. Upon T.C.'s arrival, he was shunned and not granted permission to see the General. The angry Georgia soldiers and the mob of Raleigh citizens were too many for T.C. and the other provost guards to handle. T.C. reported back to his commanding officer, Captain Waters, who then reported the situation to Governor Zeb Vance.

Seeing the perilous situation in the Capital City, Governor Vance sent a telegraph to President Davis, asking for assistance in stopping the rioting. Governor Vance expressed his indignation that Officers of the State of Georgia would have such disdain for the laws of the State of North Carolina. Vance also indicated that he would have any editor of a newspaper arrested should the paper commit treason against the Confederacy.

The rioting stopped only after President Davis sent in a contingent of Alabama soldiers on September 11 to restore order. T.C. was amazed at the actions of both the soldiers and the citizens. However, he supported and admired the actions of both Governor Vance and President Davis in how they handled the situation in such a swift manner.

On February 3, 1864, seven months after arriving in Raleigh, T.C. was summoned to the quarters of Captain Samuel Waters. Not knowing the reason for his summons, T.C. was somewhat apprehensive as he entered the quarters. After T.C. gave the standard salute, Captain Waters invited him to sit down. After some inquiries about T.C.'s military assignments and his family, Waters then stated, "Private Reavis, I have some news for you. Your service and loyalty to the Confederacy has been duly noted. Accordingly, as of today, you are being promoted to the rank of Sergeant."

T.C. was taken by surprise with the news. Not knowing what to say, he simply replied, "Thank you, Sir!" After being dismissed, Sergeant Reavis returned to his quarters and immediately wrote a letter home telling of the promotion.

A major event that T.C. experienced after being promoted was an episode in June 1864. The camp had a holding compound for soldiers who were on short-term arrest, as well as for prisoners who were awaiting transfer to either Andersonville Prison in Georgia, Castle Thunder in Richmond, or the Salisbury Prison in North Carolina. The Salisbury Prison was where captured spies were sent, as well as Confederates who were court-martialed. On the night of June 21, 1864, the guards at the compound were overpowered by fourteen deserters. The guards made little effort to make pursuit, as the physical condition of the guards provided them little or no chance to overcome the escapees.

Upon Sergeant Reavis learning of the escape, he compiled a contingent of able-bodied guards with horses and made pursuit. Based upon a tip from one of the prisoners who had not escaped, the posse headed toward Neuse Crossing. Assuming the escapees would be traveling north along the railroad tracks, T.C. had a hunch to look underneath the train trestle that crossed the Neuse River. Sure enough, eight of the escapees were found hiding there and were recaptured. The other six were nowhere to be found. T.C. called the pursuit off, as he figured it must be God's sovereign will that the six escaped, perhaps the answer to someone's prayer back home up North.

A week later, on June 29, T.C. learned that another Provost Guard camp under Mallett's Battalion, Camp Vance in Morganton, had been burned. The entire camp, except for the hospital, was burned by a band of raiders under the renegade Captain George Kirk. Captain Kirk had formed a voluntary regiment of Union soldiers comprised of North Carolinians from Burnsville. These Union Loyalists were often labeled "bushwhackers." Kirk's raiders also included Negros, Indians, and deserters.

Sergeant Reavis advised his men of the episode that had occurred at Camp Vance and placed Camp Holmes on high alert. This renegade group was one that T.C. hoped he would not have to encounter.

While T.C. was not experiencing front-line battle fighting, he was experiencing a variety of dangerous encounters nearly every day as a provost guard. He performed the duties assigned to him, but was determined to do so in an honorable fashion, treating the unfortunate prisoners and deserters he had custody of with the respect they were due.

Chapter 22 – Greys on Glebe Road

The year 1865 arrived and the war which had begun in May of 1861, and which supposedly was to last no more than six months was still underway. Both the Union and the Confederacy were still confident that their respective side could win the war. The status of the Reavis boys was as follows: Private Alex Wortham had died in September 1864 after being confined at Point Lookout in Maryland for ten months; Private Sam Reavis was still confined at Point Lookout, after having arrived there in September 1864; and Sergeant T.C. Reavis was detailed as a provost guard in the Capital City of Raleigh after having arrived there in July 1863.

The Twenty-Third Regiment, of which Sam and T.C. had enlisted, continued fighting without the two brothers. After the capture of Sam in September of 1864, the regiment fought in the Battles of Fisher's Hill, Cedar Creek, Hatcher's Run, Fort Steadman, Saylor's Creek, and Appomattox Court House.

By early March of 1865, there were so many men, mostly conscripts, deserting from Lee's Army and passing southward through North Carolina, that the Confederate authorities sought to check the desertion. One way of checking it was to position a cordon of troops across their route. For a period of three weeks, the Twenty-Third was assigned the duty of guarding roads and ferries along the border of North Carolina and Virginia, to catch the many deserters. The cordon stretched from Clarksville, Virginia to Gaston, North Carolina.

With the cordon being not too far from Glebe Road in Granville County, members of the regiment were frequently seen passing the Reavis House. Some were patrolling while some were furloughing in Henderson. The circular rock steps caught the attention of many of the soldiers passing by. On several occasions, the soldiers stopped by the house to inspect the cellar, looking for deserters that may be hiding there. The Reavis family members were always cordial to the soldiers, offering them water from the covered well. The apple orchard along the roadside also attracted the passing soldiers.

Once a visiting soldier who may have known either Sam or T.C. learned that the Reavis House was the home of one of their comrades, the soldier would always share with the family whatever camp or battle experience he may have had with them. The soldiers were saddened to hear that Sam had been incarcerated at Point Lookout for the past six months, but happy to hear that T.C. was doing well as a provost guard in Raleigh.

Mary Reavis would show the visiting soldiers the grave of her nephew, Frank McCraw, Jr., who was buried in the family cemetery. Frank, also a member of the Twenty-Third, had been killed by friendly fire at the Battle of Cedar Creek on October 19, 1864. This was just one month after Sam Reavis had been captured while on picket at Winchester. Frank was survived by his wife Betsy Wiggins McCraw, daughter of Thomas and Lucy Wiggins. The family was fortunate to have Frank's body shipped back home for burial, as Betsy's parents were financially able to pay the $300 transportation fee.

Frank was buried adjacent to his grandparents, Thomas and Lucy Coghill, who each had a fairly impressive tombstone. While there was not yet a tombstone for Frank, Mary hoped that one day there would be some type of marker for the grave. Not many of the soldiers had known Frank, since he only enlisted as a conscript in November 1863, three months after the Battle of Gettysburg. He had been a member of the regiment for less than a year. All of the soldiers however paid their respects as they visited the gravesite. A few who had actually known Frank visited his grieving twenty-four-year-old widow Betsy to give their condolences.

Two favorite stopping spots for the soldiers were the Harris Mill Pond and Stark's Mill Pond, both situated on Anderson Swamp Creek which ran across the way from the Reavis House. While the nineteen-year old Ella and thirteen-year old Mary enjoyed seeing the passing soldiers and getting their attention, their mother had forbidden them from frequenting the two mills. This was because the soldiers were often seen bathing there.

John Billie, who was now sixteen years old, was intrigued with the soldiers and struck up as many conversations as he could. Since John Billie was only ten months away from being eligible to be constricted into the Confederate Army, he was hoping to enlist in the Twenty-Third when the time came.

Near the end of March, the Twenty-Third left the Carolinas. It was summoned to Petersburg to help defend that city, participating in the Battle of Fort Steadman on March 25. Meanwhile, Union General Sherman was marching through the Carolinas, after completing his "March to the Sea Campaign." The campaign had started with the burning of Atlanta and ended with the capture of Savannah.

Sherman's Army was now marching northward to join up with General Grant's Army in Virginia. Sherman applied the principles of "scorched earth," ordering his troops to burn crops, kill livestock and consume supplies. Additionally, he destroyed civilian infrastructure along his path of advance, including mansions, grain mills, railroad depots, and factories.

Up until this time, Lewis and Mary Reavis were hopefully optimistic that the Confederate Army would win the war. They hoped that their two sons would come home, although they had already lost a son-in-law to the cause. However, having learned of the destruction that Sherman's Army had done across the South, their optimism was now turning to pessimism. This was because they saw that Sherman had destroyed much of the South's potential and will to continue waging war.

News was that Sherman was heading northward, which caused Lewis and Mary to fear that their homestead would be in his pathway. The approaching Sherman's Army would be much more devastating than any approaching hurricane.

They were also disturbed by news stories reporting the rapes of Southern women by Yankee soldiers. In many cases, Federal officers turned their heads when learning of many of the atrocities committed by the privates. The rape of a fifty-eight year old woman in Goldsboro did however result in the court martial of the offending Yankee soldier. It was reported that the convicted soldier faced a firing squad of twenty-four men. Twelve of the men had live bullets in their guns while twelve had blanks.

This pessimistic and fearful attitude of Lewis and Mary was fostered further when they learned of a letter that Sherman had written to the Chief of Army Staff. The letter stated in part, "We are not only fighting armies, but a hostile people, and must make old and young, rich and poor, feel the hard hand of war, as well as their organized armies. I know that this recent movement of mine through Georgia has had a wonderful effect in this respect. Thousands who had been deceived by their lying papers into the belief that we were being whipped all the time, realized the truth, and have no appetite for a repetition of the same experience."

The sixty-one year old Lewis Reavis had done his best to keep the farm going over the past four years. But with the slaves having been freed in 1863, and his two sons and son-in-law not being around to help with the crops, very little farm income was coming in. Inflation was running rampant. A barrel of flour that sold for eighteen dollars in 1862 and for thirty-six dollars in 1863 was now selling for an astonishing five hundred dollars.

Whatever savings Lewis had accumulated was near depletion. With the fall of the Confederacy, the Confederate currency would be worthless. Seeing how devastating the war had been on the family's lifestyle and stability, both Lewis and his wife Mary were now wishing that the war would soon end, regardless of who would be the victor.

Their despair was echoed in a letter Wesley Whitfield Reavis showed them that he had received from a cousin who was fighting near Petersburg. Oddly enough, the letter was dated April 9, the same day Lee surrendered at Appomattox. An excerpt from the letter stated, "I reckon Richmond and Petersburg will be taken and I think all of the Confederacy soon will be and I do not care how soon it has to be taken. I am wishing for the Yankees to come along here any day for I do not want to see the Confederate army no more and I hate the idea of deserting, but if the army has to leave Virginia, I shall stay behind for I can see no use in fighting anymore and I think there has been poor men enough killed for rich men's prosperity."

Upon coming to the realization that the South may very well lose the war, Mary's often-quoted statement seemed more true than ever: "I've never seen a bird fly so high yet, that every once in a while he didn't have to come down to dust his tail feathers."

Chapter 23 – Last Ditch Effort

When General Sherman passed through Columbia, South Carolina in February 1865, his army burned most of the city, including the State Capitol. After leaving the city, Sherman's Army headed northward toward Raleigh. As Sherman's Army crossed into North Carolina in March, the Union troops were divided into two wings, both marching toward the town of Goldsboro.

Confederate General Robert E. Lee had ordered General Joseph E. Johnston to concentrate all available forces to intercept Sherman's Army. The interception was to take place near Bentonville. Among the available troops ordered to assist in intercepting Sherman's Army were the sixty-five provost guards detailed at Camp Holmes in Raleigh.

On March 18, Sergeant T.C. Reavis led the convoy of guards toward Bentonville. Upon the convoy's arrival at Bentonville, General Johnston recognized the poor physical condition of the guards. Doubting their ability to fight, he sent them to Smithfield to guard the railroad depot.

During the three days of March 19-21, the Battle of Bentonville transpired, mostly in the pouring rain. The Confederates were successful the first day of the battle as they routed one of the Federal wings. However, on the next day the other Federal flank arrived, and the Union forces overwhelmed the Confederates. The 80,000 troops under Sherman's command were just too many for the 20,000 Confederates to stop. Johnston's surviving Confederate troops were forced to retreat to Smithfield. T.C. learned of the outcome of the battle when the dejected soldiers arrived at the train depot. Sherman continued on to Goldsboro and now had a clear uncontested path to Raleigh.

With news of the unfavorable outcome of the Battle of Bentonville, Sergeant T.C. Reavis and his provost guards headed back to Camp Holmes in Raleigh. They had no sooner arrived when on March 25 Major Mallett ordered an evacuation of the camp. Most of the guards were relocated to Camp Stokes in Greensboro. However, T.C. and a small contingent of men remained behind, to be at the beck and call of Governor Zeb Vance.

On April 12, the army of nearly 100,000 well supplied Union troops was camped on the large hill southwest of Raleigh. The hill, covered with majestic oaks, was the location of the State's "Insane Hospital," built in 1856. The demented patients were hopeful that they were all going to be set free by the invading troops. One of the patients did in fact convince the Federals to release him, claiming that he was locked up there only because he was a political prisoner.

Recognizing the inevitable, Governor Zeb Vance sent an envoy comprised of two former governors to negotiate with Sherman. His hopes were to avoid the City of Raleigh being burned like the South Carolina Capital of Columbia. One of the former governors was David Swain, now the President of the University of North Carolina in Chapel Hill. Swain had a high interest in preventing Sherman from burning the town of Chapel Hill as well. Sherman finally met the delegation on the evening of April 12 and agreed that Raleigh would be spared if the Union troops met no resistance. The mayor of Raleigh surrendered the city the next day, and the Union forces occupied the city.

While the negotiations were taking place south of the city, Governor Vance saw the need to remove sensitive government records from the State Capitol before Sherman occupied the city. Unfortunately, some of the Governor's aides were not as loyal as he had hoped and deserted him, fearing for their own lives. The Governor was able to call on Sergeant T.C. Reavis and his small contingent of provost guards to assist him in boxing up the records.

Around midnight on April 12, Governor Vance, his family, and the provost guards left town, passing through Cary and Hillsborough. Vance went on to Charlotte to meet with President Jefferson Davis, who on April 2 had evacuated the Confederate Capital of Richmond. Sergeant Reavis and the provost guards transported the records to an undisclosed location in Greensboro for safekeeping

With news that General Lee had surrendered at Appomattox on April 9, General Johnston met with Sherman at Bennett Place in Durham on April 17 to negotiate a surrender of his troops, which was finalized on April 26.

With General Johnston having surrendered, the Confederates were now in essence considered prisoners of the U.S. Army. At eight o'clock on the morning of May 1,

1865, Sergeant T.C. Reavis was among the first 1,000 out of approximately 30,000 in line at the Britton House Hotel in Greensboro seeking a parole offered by Federal authorities. By mid-morning T.C. had filled out and signed the required form. Those accepting their paroles were to be "peaceably disposed of and invited to return to their homes and resume their industrial pursuits."

Having received their paroles, on May 3rd the Confederate troops performed their final mustering out ceremonies. General Joseph Johnston stood on top of a wagon so all could hear him. His speech was emotional. His final words were, "Men, discharge the obligations of good and peaceful citizens at your homes as well as you have performed the duties of thorough soldiers in the field."

Upon hearing the farewell address, T.C. felt a sense of relief. There would be no more picket duty, no more guard duty, no more fighting, no more war. It was all over and he was going home to his wife Bettie and daughter Cora.

Before leaving, General Johnston ordered a portion of the Confederate Treasury that was under his custody, which was in the form of Mexican silver dollars, to be handed out among the troops. To each officer and enlisted man present was given one dollar and fourteen cents.

For many of the men, getting home meant long journeys to Texas, Louisiana, and Arkansas. For T.C. however, home was less than one hundred miles away. Like many others, he started walking, and was fortunate to be able to do so.

Chapter 24 – Bluecoats on Glebe Road

With the surrender of General Lee at Appomattox on April 9, 1865, and of General Johnston at Durham on April 26, for all practical purposes the war was now over. The assignation of President Lincoln at Ford's Theatre on April 14 and the capture of President Jefferson Davis on May 10 in Georgia marked the end of these men's leadership of the Federal Government and of the former Confederate Government.

Early Sunday morning on April 30, Sherman's Army left Raleigh, heading toward Washington. The goal was to arrive in the Federal Capital in time to march in the "Grand Review of the Armies," a celebration parade to be held on May 23. To avoid a bottleneck, the 100,000 troops left in waves. Additionally, they took different routes out of Raleigh. Some of the troops took the road toward Oxford, some the road toward Louisburg, and some the road toward Henderson. On average, each wave covered 35 miles each day before stopping to camp overnight.

At the end of the first day of marching, the first wave of troops heading toward Henderson arrived in Kittrell. This was the hometown of Colonel C.C. Blacknall, the fallen hero of the NC Twenty-Third Regiment. Kittrell was also the hometown of Corporal James T. Stone of the Regiment.

Many of the Federals took up occupation in the Kittrell Springs Hotel, the establishment that belonged to the Blacknall Family, and now being operated by Colonel Blacknall's wife Virginia. Virginia was affectionately known by the town folks as "Jinny." Just months earlier, the hotel had served as a Confederate hospital for over 300 men, with the graves of 54 Confederate soldiers who died there being located nearby. When Jinny saw the soldiers in the lobby of the hotel her heart was broken. This was because she knew her husband would turn over in his grave if he knew Yankees had taken over his establishment.

To the surprise of everyone, the Union troops were more cordial than expected. Knowing that the war was now over, the troops were relieved to know they no longer were under the mandate to "burn and destroy." Instead, General Sherman had given them orders that their mission was now to protect instead of to destroy. Sherman's proclamation was that, "All good and peaceable citizens will be protected and treated with kindness, while those who disturb the peace, or violate the laws, will be punished with the severity of martial law." Nevertheless, Jinny and her ten-year old son Oscar had made sure that all of the hotel's silverware was hidden.

Early the following morning, the Union troops left Kittrell and resumed their marching northward. Around mid-morning, the first of the troops reached Chalk Level, passing by the Reavis Tavern located there. While most of the troops kept along the main road that followed the Raleigh and Gaston Railroad toward Middleburg, several companies veered to the left and traveled along Glebe Road, taking the shortcut that led through Townesville toward Clarksville. Twenty minutes after passing through Chalk Level, the troops with the Stars and Stripes proudly displayed were seen approaching the Reavis House, which was one and one-half miles north of Chalk Level.

The entire Reavis Family living in the house at the time, along with the Negroes that had elected to stay on the farm, perched on the front porch and steps to watch the procession. The sight was something to see. Never in their lives had they seen so many uniformed soldiers marching together. They also had never seen cannons being drawn by mules. A number of wagons contained the wounded that were unable to walk.

Young John Billie laughed at some of the comical sights, as some of the soldiers had pets they had acquired along the way. While some of the soldiers were accompanied by dogs, several had non-traditional pets, including goats and raccoons. There were some wagons that were loaded with chickens and turkeys, all of which were squawking or gobbling. One group of soldiers consisted of Negroes, apparently former slaves who had joined the Union Army, now heading to the North to find a new way of life.

Every so often there would be a cavalry regiment, although none of the horses seemed to have any friskiness left in them. When Lewis Reavis saw the horses trudging along, he thought to himself, "There's no telling what horrors those horses have seen." He also wondered if the horses knew if the war was over and that their duty had been fulfilled.

The soldiers all seemed jubilant, even though most of their clothing looked ragged. Very few of the men wore a complete uniform. Even the ones who did have a uniform showed stitched patches. Some of the men were even bare-chested. Most did have a cap or hat, but some only had a rag tied around their head. Nearly all had beards. The officers were easily recognized, as most were on horseback.

The soldiers, marching no more than 100 yards in front of the Reavis House, were most captivating to Ella and her younger sister Mary. Young men were something the girls had not seen much of over the past four years. While her twin sister Della had married in November of 1863, Ella felt like her teen years had been short-changed. She was less than one month away from turning 20 years of age and still not married.

Soldiers just kept coming, as it appeared the procession would never end, and this was just the first wave. Along about one o'clock, orders to "halt" could be heard, as it was time for the troops to stop for a lunch break. All of the farms along Glebe Road now had Yankees squatting on the property, including the Billy Wortham farm to the south and the Thomas Hester farm to the north.

In front of the Reavis House alone, there must have been three hundred soldiers. A number of them were seeking shade under the cedar trees and under the apple trees. The soldiers were close enough to the front of the Reavis House that their conversations could easily be overheard. From the conversations, it was obvious that they had noticed the girls sitting on the circular rock steps. However, it was the cedar trees and boxwood bushes that first drew their attention to the steps on which they sat.

Noticing the audience sitting on the steps, a handful of the soldiers situated in front of the house came up the pathway toward the house. Although those sitting on the steps did not feel threatened, they still had some apprehension regarding how friendly the soldiers might be. Out of precaution, Lewis Reavis had removed the Confederate Flag that normally hung from the roof of the covered well. Mary Reavis had made sure that any of the family's valuables were hidden in the cellar. Although the cellar had easy access, there was a hidden section that would have been difficult for even the most astute searcher to find.

When the soldiers reached the black walnut tree in the front yard, they stopped. One spoke up and addressed Lewis Reavis, who had stepped forward as the soldiers approached. "Sir, we mean no harm to you or your family. We will respect your property while we take a temporary break from the heat. We did notice the covered well and would be ever grateful if we could draw some fresh water, as that in our canteens seems to be stale."

Lewis Reavis figured that their story was likely a ploy to get a closer look at the girls. Nevertheless, he complied and gave them permission to draw a bucket of water. The two sisters could not refrain from giggling as they watched the soldiers trying to figure out how to draw the water from the well. The soldiers seemed to fumble at the task, either because they did not know how to manage the pulley and chain, or because they were too mesmerized by the pretty girls.

One of the soldiers had the need to relieve himself. Noticing the johnny house close by, he took the liberty of visiting the facility. The johnny house was a "two-holer," as Mary had her husband build it that way shortly after the twins were born. This was the first known time that a Yankee had ever frequented the johnny house on the Reavis farm. Later that day, John Billie would find the following inscription carved on the inside of the door, "47th Ohio was here – May 1, 1865."

Still a little leery of the soldiers' intentions, Lewis started a dialogue with them. To Lewis's surprise, the boys were no different than his own sons, just wearing different colored uniforms. They told Lewis about how they had volunteered four years earlier, and how they missed their homes and family back up North. Lewis even discovered that they knew and worshiped the same Jesus that he did. It was evident that they were glad the war was over and that they could now stop fighting their fellow countrymen. Before the soldiers left, Mary came out the back door and gave each one an apple jack. The expression of satisfaction Mary saw on the soldiers' faces as they ate the Southern delicacy warmed her heart.

The soldiers then headed on back down the pathway, just in time to join the troops as they continued their journey northward. When nightfall came, another wave of soldiers arrived. This wave made camp in the apple orchard in front of the house. That night, the singing of songs and hymns could be heard around the campfires, until orders for lights to be out were given around nine o'clock.

Early the next morning, this wave of troops moved on. This cycle of marching and camping continued for the next two days as more waves passed by the house. Altogether, there must have been 15,000 soldiers that passed the house over the first three days of May in 1865. Mary Reavis was kept busy frying apple jacks for any of the soldiers who ventured up the path to see the rock steps.

Chapter 25 – Coming Home

By May 4, 1865, the last of the waves of Yankees leaving Raleigh and marching to Washington had passed the Reavis House on Glebe Road. However, throughout the summer and into the fall, there would be small contingents of Union troops charged with patrolling the county to keep martial law.

It was planting time and yet not all of the fields had been plowed, although the tobacco beds had plenty of seedlings ready to be transplanted. Lewis Reavis assembled the handful of Negroes that had stuck with him and divided up the work to be performed. Young John Billie, the only son available to help, was given the assignment of plowing the field at the "Low Place," which was along Indian Creek.

It had been over two months since there had been any word from either of the two sons who had gone off to war. The last word was that Sam was an inmate at Point Lookout in Maryland, and that T.C. was a provost guard in Raleigh, if not killed at the Battle of Bentonville. While Lewis and Mary had previously learned the tragic fate of their son-in-law Alex

Wortham, they prayed every day for the safe return of their two sons, for whom there was still hope.

While Lewis was mostly out working in the fields, Mary spent nearly all her time sitting on the front porch eagerly hoping that one of the many soldiers she saw walking along Glebe Road would be one of her sons to turn up the pathway to the house. Bettie Reavis, Mary's daughter-in-law, would frequently help keep watch. Many times as the women sat on the porch, there would be a jack rabbit sitting on the bottom of the circular rocks steps, seemingly watching as well.

What the Reavis Family did not know was that T.C. had avoided the Battle of Bentonville and had gone to Greensboro with Governor Vance. They also did not know that T.C. left Greensboro on May 3, after being paroled on May 1. Being 100 miles away, it would take him three days to walk home.

Neither did the Reavis Family know that Sam had been pardoned from Point Lookout on March 18 and later exchanged at Aiken Landing on the James River. Yet, the family had not received any word from Sam regarding his release. After being exchanged, Sam had elected to remain in Richmond, primarily because he was too weak to travel. While he did not require to be hospitalized for his touch of dysentery, he was among several released inmates that took up boarding in an abandoned house. The house was owned by Phoebe Yates Pember, matron of Chimborazo Hospital nurses. Sam remained there recuperating until April 2, when it was apparent that Richmond would be overrun by Union Forces.

Fearful that he would once again be captured, even though he was still weak, Sam embarked upon his long journey home. He left Richmond just before the city was torched by the invading Yankees. The route he chose was toward Danville, Virginia, the same route planned to be taken by President Jefferson Davis and his cabinet. In fact, it was at the train station that Sam saw George Davis, the Confederate Attorney General from Wilmington supervising the loading of several trunks into a railroad car. Recognizing George Davis as being a fellow Tar Heel, Sam offered to assist in loading the trunks. Sam was not told what was in the trunks, which were awfully heavy. He suspected the contents must have been very valuable, as each trunk had double padlocks. Attorney General Davis thanked Sam for assisting in the task and told him he hoped to see him in Carolina.

While President Davis and his cabinet left for Danville by train, Sam would take out on foot. Most of Sam's travels were at night, in order to avoid being captured by Union forces patrolling major roads looking for stragglers. While it took T.C. three days to travel home from Greensboro, it would take Sam thirty-five days to travel home from Richmond, after taking a brief stopover in Danville.

Sam spent several days in Danville, spending some of the time searching for the portion of the Confederate Treasury that was rumored to have been hidden there. He knew he would recognize the trunks if he saw them, now having figured out what was in the trunks he helped load at the Richmond train station.

Back in Granville County, it was now three o'clock on Saturday afternoon, May 6. Mary Reavis and Bettie Reavis were both sitting on the front porch, vigilantly watching for any sign of the two Reavis brothers. One of the family's dogs that was getting up in age was lying on the porch, making strange moaning sounds. Mary recognized the moaning and commented to Bettie, "Old Yellow is just too lazy to get up off of that nail he's lying on." Bettie just chuckled.

As fate would have it, the two Reavis brothers the women were looking out for were each on Glebe Road, but at opposite ends. T.C. had passed through Chalk Level and was heading north on the road, while Sam on the other hand had passed through Townesville and was heading south on the road.

There were many Confederate refugees traveling the road, and from a distance nearly all of them looked alike to the Reavis women. With nearly all of the soldiers passing by having beards, recognizing someone would be difficult unless they were right upon you.

Bettie was the first to spot a soldier walking up the path toward the house along the row of cedar trees leading toward Chalk Level. Almost at the same time, Mary spotted another soldier walking up the path along the row of cedar trees leading toward Greystone. Each of the women was looking in different directions down the two paths that led to the house, not realizing that the other woman was also spying a soldier that was a prospective Reavis.

As each soldier drew closer, the women's emotions began to run wild. They both thought to themselves, but were too scared to verbalize: "Could it be? Could this be T.C. or Sam? If it is, what do I do? Do I run to meet him, or do I go first and get the family? If it is not one of them, can I stand the disappointment?"

It seemed as if the two soldiers approaching from two different angles were being drawn to the circular rock steps like a magnet, and unless stopped would arrive at the vertex at the same time. However, by the time the soldiers were each within 25 yards of the porch, each woman knew without a doubt at whom they were looking. Simultaneously, the women both screamed and ran down the steps toward their respective focal point. It was only when the jack rabbit that had been sitting on the steps ran between the two soldiers that everyone realized there were actually two Reavis brothers now home on sacred ground.

By this time, the rest of the family had converged on the soldiers in the yard, as the family members had come from the house and the fields to see what all the commotion was about. Talking about a hallelujah breakdown, there was a big one right there in broad daylight.

Chapter 26 – Five Sisters

While the past four years had been mostly focused on the Reavis men who were off at war, the five Reavis sisters - Martha, Lucy, Ella, Della, and Mary - had taken somewhat of a back seat.

June 29, 1865 was the twentieth birthday of the twin girls, Ella and Della. It was almost five years to the day that the census taker had visited the Reavis House on Glebe Road in 1860. There were times when the twin girls felt neglected, although they knew they were loved dearly by their parents. Nearly all of the twins' teenage years had been spent under the cloud of war. There was little opportunity for romance since boys their age were scarce. Also, with the slaves having been freed in January 1863, the twins had to take on chores they were not use to performing.

One night after the twins had a spat, as siblings sometimes do, their mother sat them down for a talk. Mary reminded the twins of the scripture that talked about the fruit of the spirit, with the greatest being love. Realizing love was not an easy concept to comprehend, Mary told them that demonstration of love between family members requires putting two virtues into action: respect for the other, and gratitude for what the other has done for them.

Mary picked up a candle to use as an illustration. "Girls, this candle consists of both wax and a wick. Wax without a wick is no candle, and a wick without wax is no candle. Likewise, love cannot be demonstrated without both respect and gratitude. As we all know, without the light that a candle produces, there is darkness."

Seeing the puzzlement on the twins' faces, Mary continued, "The glue that ties the two virtues together is forgiveness. Forgiveness is a form of medicine, as it allows us to release any negative feelings we may have toward another."

Ella asked, "But what if the other person does not deserve to be forgiven?"

Mary smiled and responded, "We must forgive, even when the wrong the other person has committed does not from a human perspective merit it. The Bible calls it grace. The motivation for forgiving is our desire to be obedient to Christ." It was wisdom like this that created and kept a close bond between the two girls, even into their adult years.

Throughout the war, Ella had been corresponding with Private John Jeremiah Pegram of Warren County's Sandy Creek, a fellow she had met at church before the war started. It was not love at first sight, but love that grew at a distance. Three years older than Ella, John was eighteen years old when he enlisted in the NC Thirtieth Regiment in August of 1861. While some of John's correspondence was written from the battlefield, some was written from prison and some from a hospital.

John Jeremiah had been taken as prisoner two different times, the first time at Frederick, Maryland in September 1862, and the second time at Kelly's Ford in November 1863. In fact, when he was captured the second time, he was imprisoned at Point Lookout along with Alex Wortham, Ella's brother-in-law. John Jeremiah's stay at Point Lookout was for just over five months, before being part of a prisoner exchange in April 1864. It was during a four-month stay at home that spring that he called on his sweetheart and pen pal.

But by the end of August, he felt his duty was to return to his regiment to continue fighting for the cause. Five months later, John Jeremiah was wounded in the left arm at Petersburg and hospitalized in Richmond's Moore Hospital. In February of 1865, after having his forearm amputated, he was furloughed and returned to Warren County.

June 29, 1865 could very well have been Ella's best birthday, for in two days, on July 1, she would become John Jeremiah's bride. Now that Ella's two brothers were home from the war, and John Billie was a teenager, she no longer felt an obligation to remain home with her parents. It was now her time to be in the spotlight. A stunning wedding it would be. Ella was proud to be marrying a Confederate veteran. The fact that he only had one arm made him that more special to her. She often kidded him about having to wear his wedding ring on his right hand.

Although Ella's brother Sam was present at the house wedding, Sam's mind was miles away, as it was the second anniversary of that dreadful day at Gettysburg. This was the place where most of his comrades of the Twenty-Third Regiment were struck down before him, and where he had to crawl for his life to Iverson's Pit. July the 1st would be an awful day of remembrance for the rest of his life.

A year-and-a-half earlier, the other twin, Della, had married George Brittain Harris. George's family owned and operated Harris Mill. Situated on Anderson Swamp Creek, the mill was a little over one mile from the Reavis House. Della and George were hoping to start a family, but it would be six more years before such a blessing would come along.

Della's given birth name was actually "Ardella," and Ella's given birth name was actually "Arella." In Hebrew, Ardella means "blooming meadow;" and Arella means "messenger from God, or angel."

Lucy Reavis Wortham was by far the sister who had the most difficult time during the war. For the first year of the war, her husband Alex stayed home serving as the farm's overseer, before he enlisted in 1862. During the next two years however, Lucy would have to deal with the agony associated with wondering if her husband was safe and if he would survive the war. For ten months of that time, her distress was magnified with the knowledge that Alex was incarcerated in a Maryland prison. The only windows of relief for Lucy were the two times Alex was home on sick furlough, with one of those times being when their only child Pattie was conceived.

Grief was overwhelming when Lucy learned of Alex's death in September of 1864. Lucy's hope for the future was sustained by her faith in God. Additionally, hope grew as the result of the blessing she received through caring for her daughter. Pattie was born only three weeks before Alex was taken prisoner in November 1863. Being a single mother in the years following the war would be Lucy's biggest challenge. Being able to live in the Reavis House with her parents would be a blessing, not only to her, but to her parents as well.

One night while sitting on the front porch feeling somewhat depressed, Lucy asked her father the question, "Why have all these terrible things happened to our family?" Lewis thought for a moment and then responded, "Lucy, some people think that life is a problem to be solved, but it's not. It's a mystery to be lived."

Not understanding her father's answer, Lucy asked, "But why is there so much pain and sorrow?"

Lewis responded, "As we go through life, we will bear pain. We just have to be careful that we are not the ones who inflict pain upon others. When you find yourself feeling weary and wishing things were different, do not be ashamed of your state of exhaustion. Those are the times you should view as opportunities to pause and develop a closer relationship with the Lord." Lucy took these words of encouragement to heart and passed the wisdom on to her daughter whenever she encountered trials and tribulations of her own.

Martha Vaughan, the oldest of the five Reavis sisters had been kept busy raising her three children, Nora, Belle, and John. She still grieved the loss of her first child who had only lived three days. She visited her infant daughter's grave in the family cemetery frequently. However, Martha had experienced a difficult birth when her son John was born in March of 1863, during the height of the war. She had been sickly ever since, giving her husband John much concern. It was the fall of 1866 when Martha unexpectedly passed away, with heart failure being the suspected cause of death. Martha had known that her deceased daughter could not be brought back to her. Instead, Martha had comfort in knowing that one day she would join her daughter in heaven.

Martha's husband John Vaughan was a merchant in Henderson at the time and was finding it difficult to care for a three-year old, a six-year old, and an eight-year old. While Martha had died at the early age of thirty-one, John was fifty-one years old at the time, twenty years her elder. Being grandparents, Lewis and Mary Reavis helped out as much as possible, with their youngest daughter Mary providing much of the children's care. It was then that John Vaughan approached the grandparents and made a most unusual request. John asked for their permission to marry their youngest daughter Mary, who was only fourteen at the time, thirty-seven years his junior.

John was almost in tears as he gave the reasons for his request, "I miss Martha greatly and will always have a place for her in my heart. The children also miss her greatly. I feel guilty for them not having a mother. However, for the past six months that Mary has been helping care for them, they are beginning to see her as a mother figure. I admire your daughter Mary and have respect for the maturity she has shown in honoring her sister's dying request to take care of the children. Every time I look at Mary, I see Martha, as their features and dispositions are so much the same. It is as though Martha's spirit lives on through Mary. If you will honor this request, and Mary will agree, I promise to be the best husband I can be to your daughter, and the best father I can be to your grandchildren."

Lewis and Mary listened intently, and told John that they would consider his request and let him know their decision the next day. As Lewis and his wife Mary discussed it that night, they both admitted that the possibility had previously crossed their minds. The proposal was a custom that had been practiced by some in the South. As they knelt on their knees that night to say their prayers, they asked for wisdom and revelation of God's will in the matter.

The next morning after breakfast, young Mary was sitting on the front steps. She was dressing two corn husk dolls that she intended to give her nieces. Lewis and Mary went out and sat with her. Upon revealing John Vaughan's request to her, young Mary's eyes just glowed, showing excitement over the proposal. It wasn't clear if the excitement was over becoming a wife or becoming an instant mother.

Lewis and Mary had a peace about them as they made their decision to support the proposal. They had come to the joint conclusion that by letting Mary go, they themselves would be in a better position to hold on to the hand of the Lord. Their only request was that the wedding be delayed until July of 1867, at which time young Mary would then be fifteen years old.

Mary did express her concern to Lewis about what the neighbors might think. Lewis recognized her concern and told her, "Any fool can criticize, and most fools do."

Arella "Ella" and Ardella "Della" Reavis (Twins)

Chapter 27 – Life Goes On

While the war had ended, it was evident to Lewis and Mary Reavis that life would continue to go on, just not in the same manner as it did before the war. Like most other Southern planters, the value of their assets had plummeted. When the census taker came in 1870, while the value of their real estate had remained at $6,000, the value of their personal property had dropped from $19,800 to $1,000. Not only had they lost their slaves, but inflation during the Reconstruction era was taking a toll as well. Considered a wealthy family before the war, they were now "just farmers" trying to survive in a world that depended largely on the labor of the family members and hired help.

During the Reconstruction years, the Radical Republicans in Congress distrusted ex-Confederates and enacted hash policies in order to punish the former Rebels. Ella and John Jeremiah Pegram experienced first-hand the consequences of dealing with the Carpetbaggers. The Pegrams had acquired interest in land upon which the granite quarry at Greystone was to be excavated. However, through some legal maneuvering, the family was swindled out of the property. This was an episode that would be a thorn in the side of the Reavises and Pegrams for years to come.

Lewis Reavis had no use for the Radicals, the Carpetbaggers from the North, or the Scalawags in the South who supported the Radicals. This was no more evident than one day during the Presidential Election of 1868 when Lewis was in Henderson and had a political discussion with Mr. Barnes of Bear Pond. As relayed by a distant cousin Thurston Titus Hicks, Lewis was supposedly overheard saying, "Barnes, when I die and go to Heaven, Saint Peter will meet me at the gate and hold out his hand and say: 'Come in Reavis.' And I will say to him: 'Peter, are there any Radicals in Heaven?' And if he says yes, I'll say, 'Well, take me back to Chalk Level.' "

Obviously, Lewis was sorely disappointed when Democratic Horatio Seymour lost the election to Republican Ulysses Grant. Mary reminded Lewis that nothing in heaven had changed, as Jesus was still on the throne. Thereafter, whenever he opened his gold pocket watch, he was reminded, "This too shall pass!"

The two Reavis boys who were not married when the war ended would eventually marry. In March of 1869, after having survived the war and then being single for four years thereafter, Sam Reavis married Sallie Margaret Basket of the Spring Valley Community. Three years later in 1872, John Billie married Sallie's younger sister, Rebecca. So when the census of 1880 was taken, only Lucy and her eighteen-year old daughter Pattie were living at home with Lewis and Mary Reavis on Glebe Road.

In the case of Lucy Reavis Wortham, who had become a widow as a result of the war, for the longest time it appeared she would never marry again. But in 1881, seventeen years after Alex had died, a suitor from Kittrell came calling. James T. Stone, a recent widower, had been a friend of the family since the war. In fact, Stone had been a Corporal in the Twenty-Third Regiment, the same regiment as T.C. and Sam Reavis.

Stone had many war stories to tell the forty-two year old Lucy, including the time he assisted her brother Sam in carrying T.C. off of the Sunken Road at Sharpsburg when T.C. had been wounded. He also told of the day at the Battle of Chancellorsville when he played possum to keep from being captured by the Yankees. However, Stone's most colorful story was the day he himself was wounded in the hip at the Battle of Gettysburg, and taken prisoner the same day. After being exchanged from prison, Stone served for a period of time as a guard at the Confederate Hospital located in Kittrell. During the last days of the war he returned to active duty and was again taken prisoner, helping to defend the City of Petersburg. He was imprisoned at Point Lookout, the very same prison that Lucy's husband Alex had been held prisoner for ten months before he died.

When James Stone came calling on "Mrs. Lucy," because of his limp, he had a little difficulty getting up the circular rock steps at the Reavis House. To him, it was worth the effort. Stone did not appear to be the typical Confederate soldier, as he was only five-feet, five-and-three-quarter inches tall, or at least that was his recorded height when he was paroled from Point Lookout. Perhaps it was his blonde hair and blue eyes that attracted Lucy to him; or perhaps Lucy was captivated by the stories Stone told that associated him with her departed husband.

It was in a letter that the debonair Stone asked Lucy for her hand in marriage. The letter was written in broken English, as Stone had limited reading and writing skills. Even on his enlistment papers, he signed making his "mark." In the letter, he told her that he was not out for her property, and she could "stop people from talking if she would only say yes."

It could have been a double wedding, as in December of 1881 Lucy married Stone, and Lucy's daughter Pattie married Hugh Jones Reavis, a distant cousin from Sandy Plains. The Reavis House in the Silver Spring Community on Glebe Road was now fully occupied again. Not only did James Stone move in with Lucy, but Hugh Reavis moved in with Pattie as well.

Surely the motivation of these marriages was love. However, without these two men coming to the rescue, one wonders if the Reavis Family on Glebe Road would have survived the depressed economic times otherwise? On the other hand, would the defeated and demoralized men have coped with having lost the war, without the women's reassurance of their manhood?

The Silver Spring Community embraced the new Reavis Family members by inviting them to join them in their weekly worship services. In 1880 a group of local residents had begun meeting on Sundays in the school house located on the Reavis property. Along with other prominent families in the community, the Reavises were later instrumental in chartering the church to be known as the Silver Spring Methodist Protestant Church.

While life routinely goes on through marriages and births, each generation eventually comes to an end, at least on this earth. For Lewis and Mary Reavis, there was no exception. Lewis passed away on Christmas Day in 1882 at the age of 78, and Mary passed away the following December at the age of 70. No truer words have ever been spoken than those of Mary Coghill Reavis, who at every Christmas dinner had reminded her children that, "There are plenty of people here this Christmas who will not be here next Christmas."

While only God knows the eternal destiny of Lewis and Mary, Lewis left behind a clue in the form of a *Last Will and Testament*. The will states in part: "In the name of God. Amen. I, Lewis Reavis of the County of Granville NC being aware of the shortness and uncertainty of human life, and being of sound mind and disposing memory - do hereby make, publish and declare this to be my last will and testament...Item 1st - I give my body to the dust of the earth and my soul into the hands of God who gave it...."

Chapter 28 - Fragrance of Honeysuckles

The deaths of Lewis and Mary Reavis in the early 1880s marked the end of the second generation of Reavises occupying the Reavis House built in 1789. Samuel and Patsey Harris Reavis had represented the first generation of occupants. Through the lineage of daughter Lucy, there would be five more generations of Reavis occupants before the house's purpose of serving as a Reavis residence would have run its course.

As time passed, there would be minor demographical changes. With the creation of new counties in 1881, the house would then be situated in Vance County instead of Granville County. The community would be become known as Flat Rock Community instead of Silver Spring Community. Chalk Level would disappear and be replaced with a fertilizer plant. The name of the road would be changed from Glebe Road to Satterwhite Point Road. Additionally, the road would no longer extend to Townesville (now called Townsville), as the building of Kerr Lake would dissect the road.

Visitors to the Reavis House and family cemetery in future years would marvel at what they saw during their visit, but have little knowledge of the episodes that transpired there decades before. There would be many things no longer there when occupied by Lewis and Mary Reavis. Some of the things missing would be the slave quarters, the horse stables, the corn crib, the pig pens, the chicken houses, the tobacco barns, the johnny house, the smokehouse, the apple orchard, the wild cherry tree, about half of the cedar trees that had lined the two pathways, and even one of the pathways itself. One of the three chimneys would be missing, as it would fall victim to a hurricane.

There would be no evidence of the trials and hardships experienced during the Civil War, except perhaps for the gravesite of Private Frank McCraw, Jr., which would be identified by a Confederate marker placed there by the United Daughters of the Confederacy.

Behind each tombstone in the cemetery there would be a story, but no one there to tell it. Even though the inscription on Hugh Reavis' tombstone would read, "His memory is blessed," and the inscription on Lucy Reavis' tombstone would read, "Gone but not forgotten," the question that begs would be, "By whom?" Most would not know the location of the graves of Lewis and Mary Reavis, as they are marked only by two granite rocks with no inscription at all. There would be a fragrance similar to the smell of honeysuckles, but yet there would be no honeysuckles vines to be seen.

What would be remaining for the visitor to see however would be the two large boxwood bushes and the covered well. But what would grab the visitor's attention the most would be the magnificent circular rock steps in front of the house. The top rock step with the petrified water vein running through it would be a puzzle to them. Most likely, the visitor would see a jack rabbit close by the steps, if not in the cemetery. If multiple visits were made to the homeplace, the same rabbit would likely be seen each time. Just like the ancient pyramids, the circular rock steps would be weather-worn, but boy, what a story the steps would tell, if only they could talk! Or perhaps the rabbit!

Grave of Lucy Reavis
Wife of Alex Wortham and James T. Stone

ABOUT THE AUTHOR

David C. Reavis retired from North Carolina State Government as a Treasury Professional after 36 years of service. Upon his retirement in 2011, Governor Beverly Perdue bestowed upon him the "Order of the Long Leaf Pine," which is among the most prestigious awards presented by the Governor of North Carolina. In a consulting capacity he continues to function as the "E-Commerce Subject Matter Expert" for the University of North Carolina System.

David has been doing genealogy research on the Reavis Family for over 35 years, maintaining the ReavisHistory.Com website. He grew up in the Reavis Homeplace located in Vance County, NC, built by Samuel Reavis in 1789. He has always appreciated the heritage represented by the generations of Reavises who have lived there, especially during the Civil War. In writing his first historical novel, he was inspired by the resilience of the human spirit demonstrated by his ancestors who endured and survived one of the most horrific periods of America's history.

David and his wife Deelane live in Raleigh, NC and have a second home in North Myrtle Beach, SC.

BOOK WEBSITE

www.UponTheseSteps.com

Readers are encouraged to visit the book's website. Here you can find out more about the book's characters, the Reavis Homeplace, and the Granville Rifles. You can also view pictures of the circular rock steps.

Additionally, you can learn where and how to gain access to genealogy information on the Reavis and related families.

Through the website readers can contact the author, read reviews and endorsements, as well as learn about current events associated with the book and the author.

Made in the USA
Charleston, SC
03 March 2013